MW00529533

TREASURY OF FOLKLORE
SEAS & RIVERS

Dedicated to everyone who has contributed to the **#FolkloreThursday** magic over the years.

First published in the United Kingdom in 2021 by
B.T. Batsford
43 Great Ormond Street
London WC1N 3HZ

An imprint of B.T. Batsford Holdings Ltd

Illustrations by Joe McLaren

ISBN: 9781849946599

A CIP catalogue record for this book is available from the British Library.

10 9 8 7 6 5 4 3 2

Reproduction by Rival Colour, UK
Printed by Toppan Leefung Printing Ltd, China

This book can be ordered direct from the publisher at www.batsford.com, or try your local bookshop

TREASURY OF FOLKLORE
SEAS & RIVERS

DEE DEE CHAINEY &
WILLOW WINSHAM

CONTENTS

Part One

Treasures, Seduction and Death: The Lure of the Ocean Waves **6**

The Seas and Oceans **8**

Famous Floods **14**

Mermaids, Selkies and Sirens **19**

Seductress or Saviour? The Timeless Lure of the Mermaid **19**

The Little Mermaid: A Tale from Denmark **21**

The Call of the Siren **29**

The Selkie-folk, the Shapeshifting Seals of the Northern Seas **31**

From Mermaid to Serpent Queen: The Many Guises of Mami Wata **35**

The Fabled Coast of Puglia **39**

The Legend of Cristalda and Pizzomunno **39**

The Dolphin of Taranto **43**

The Priestess Io and the Ionian Sea **46**

Monsters from the Deep **47**

Scylla and Charybdis **51**

Islands of Fable and Myth **54**

Maui, Demi-God and Creator of Islands **56**

Claimed by the Waves: Underwater Worlds **59**

The Lost City of Ys **59**

The German Atlantis: The Lost City of Vineta **63**

Urashima Tarõ and the Palace of the Dragon King **65**

Scheherazade's Tales: One Thousand and One Nights **68**

The Fisherman and the Jinni **69**

The Tale of the Ensorcelled Prince **75**

Reversal of Fortune: The Lady of Stavoren **77**

Red Sky at Night: Sailor Superstitions from Across the Globe **88**

Haunting the Waves: Ghostly Ships and Skeleton Crews **90**

The Graveyard of the Atlantic: The Mystery of the Bermuda Triangle **94**

Of Coffins, Rogues and Priests: Smuggling Around England's Coasts **97**

Part Two

What Lurks Beneath: Sacred Rivers & Mysterious Lakes **102**
Rivers and Lakes **104**
Sacred Rivers **108**
Rivers of the Underworld **110**
Greek **111**
Korean **112**
Norse **113**
Forgotten Waters: The Hidden Rivers of London **114**
Waterfall Folklore **120**
The Maid of the Mist **120**
The Dragon's Gate **123**
Lover's Leap: Suicidal Lovers **125**
Oba's Ear: A Tale of the Yoruba River Spirit **126**
The Mysterious Waters of Scotland **133**
Water Horses: Majestic and Malevolent Creatures from the Depths **137**
Humped Serpents and Vicious Eels: Loch Ness and the World's Most Fearsome Lake Monsters **141**
Ogopogo **144**
Folklore or Fakelore? The Monster of Bear Lake **145**
The Folklore of Swamps and Marshes **148**
Sinister Bog Lights: Will-o'-the-Wisp **150**
Be Careful Where You Rest: The Insatiable Appetite of the Irish Joint Eater **156**
Well Folklore **157**
The Fountain of Youth **162**
Myth and Mystery: The Lady of the Lake **164**

Conclusion: What Can We Learn from Our Seas and Rivers? **167**
Acknowledgements **170**
References **172**
Index **188**

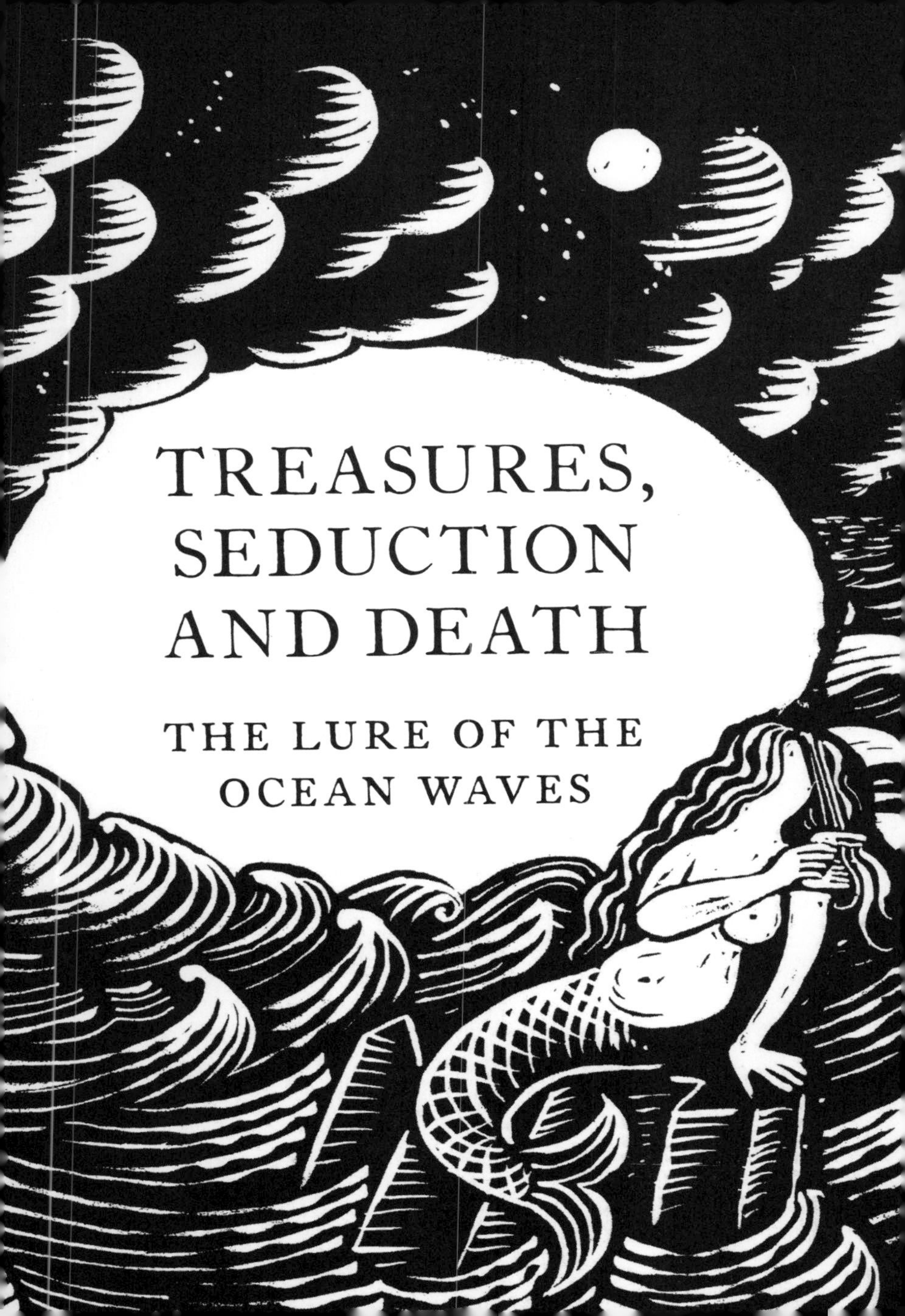
TREASURES,
SEDUCTION
AND DEATH
THE LURE OF THE
OCEAN WAVES

THE SEAS AND OCEANS

From the earliest times, the sea has been a major part of life for many people around the globe. Humans walked across continents, and traversed the seas, to settle the shores of distant lands that belonged only to the beasts of the earth. Since the ice receded, and tundra spread over our planet, island and coastal communities sprang up whose lives and livelihoods relied on the sea, as they still do today. Throughout the world, from the windy cliffs of Cornwall in England to the furthest reaches of the Philippines, we see that life on the coast is well and truly alive. Cornish folk bands, like the Fisherman's Friends of Port Isaac, sing shanties passed on by their grandfathers as they trawl the cold waves of the Celtic Sea, and they know all the stories of their shores, from Land's End to the Lizard. While far away, on the other side of the globe, Sama-Bajau fishermen watch the same sun set after their day on the waves, yet there will be no return to land for them: they reside in their boats, living a nomadic lifestyle under the ever-watching Southeast Asian skies.

From time immemorial, people have known that the sea gives life; yet we are also aware that the dark waves can take it away just as easily. In early times, the gods and goddesses of the sea were blamed for withholding food and causing death. No poem fills the soul with fear so much as *The Rime of the Ancient Mariner* – with its threat of drowning, starvation and the wrath of the gods of the ancient seas. This poem conjures the scourge that would befall sailors if they transgressed the bounds of superstition, and the well-known rules of the lore of luck, which governed their life on the ocean waves. A symbol of the subconscious mind, the sea has always ebbed and flowed. While filled with fear, danger and death, it also stirs unspoken longings for secret lovers, unbridled lust, and yearnings for another life in the bejewelled palaces of the sea. As people stare off into the curved horizon, disappearing as a watery pathway to the unknown, they dream of far-off shores and distant lands. The sea always offered an answer to the dreary lives of many who felt their lives on the land offered little more than tilling the soil while still slaves to starvation, mired in the mud of a gruelling life with the plough.

Love is often linked with the sea, and tales abound where sailors are tempted by sirens or wily mermaids. In many stories abduction masquerades as love – a constant threat to lonely youths who wander the coasts at night. Many of these are taken captive by mermen, stolen by selkies, or dragged off to Finfolkaheem, the underwater home of the sinister finmen who lurk around the shores of Orkney and Scandinavia, eagerly trying to snatch

FUNAYŪREI: THE VENGEFUL DROWNED SAILORS OF JAPAN

When out at sea on rainy days in Japan, particularly on the night of a new moon, it is wise to take precautions against Funayūrei – those remnants of drowned sailors who are still intent on taking revenge on others for their lost lives, and adventures cut short, by ladling water into boats with a view to sinking them. One must remember to always carry some *onigiri*, or rice balls, that can be thrown into the sea to ward off such horrors. If rice balls are unavailable, another solution is to prepare a *hishaku*, or water ladle used in the tea ceremony, with a missing bottom – a sure way to protect yourself from these watery fiends.

a beguiling innocent to their fate. The Blue Men of Minch are a further horror to be faced by wayward seafarers in the waters of the Outer Hebrides. Also known as storm kelpies due to their ability to rouse tempests out at sea, it's said that they wait patiently for sailors to drag beneath the waves, luring ships to their fate in the watery depths.

Yet, for others, the sea is cathartic. In many flood myths the rains come, and the overcrowded earth is submerged as the waters renew and cleanse the world of the impious and unworthy, making it ready for a new dawn of humanity. From folklore, myths and legends we can see that humanity has always viewed the sea as majestic, with a power to consume all; a regenerative, creative force that churns outside the bounds of time, roaring its way through land, animals and humans alike. In the face of this, people look at the sea with an all-consuming awe, and see the gods and goddesses of creation shimmering in its depths.

As a realm of the gods, and a source of life for many, it is unsurprising that even today people revere the ocean and give offerings to it. Hindus in Bali still submerge holy statues of gods and ancestors in the sea to purify them and imbue them with supernatural powers in a ceremony called Melasti. Similarly, Jews cast off their sins into the depths by reciting prayers and throwing breadcrumbs into the sea during Rosh Hashanah – the beginning

OFFERING FOR THE SEA IN POLYNESIA

Some communities take this idea of offerings and purification further; Polynesians will ritually dispose of umbilical cords in the sea. It's also believed that pregnant mothers should never salt or string fish.

of the Jewish new year. In Rio de Janeiro, New Year's Eve is celebrated with the festival of Iemanjá, where offerings for the goddess are sent in boats to the sea; it is believed that if she chooses to accept the offerings they will sink, and the supplicant's wishes will be granted. A similar sight can be seen annually in France, when each year people from the many Romani communities arrive in Aix-en-Provence on a pilgrimage route, in order to give offerings to their saint, Sara-la-Kali, in a procession to the ocean. On Shetland the relatively modern festival of Up Helly Aa marks their new year. There, too, huge boats are constructed – resembling Viking longships – and sent out to the sea in flames to the beating of drums and the sound of trumpets.

For thousands of years, great heroes and heroines from across the globe have traversed the seven seas, battling pirates and monsters for the prize of treasure, fame and the promise of a life of adventure and the lure of exotic shores. On their voyages, archetypal heroes are often favoured by gods of the sea and are witness to miraculous beasts, underwater worlds and palaces, and to fabled islands. One place that has been named as just such an island, time and time again, is Malta. Some say it might have been the inspiration for Atlantis due to its giant stone gantija temples, which are some of the oldest surviving remnants from the ancient world. While still disputed, others say that the Maltese island of Gozo is the fabled Ogygia, home to the sorceress Calypso. St Paul's Island, off the Maltese coast, is believed to be the place where the Apostle Paul was shipwrecked in the Bible, while on his way to Rome in around 60CE; it is said that this is how Christianity reached the shores of Malta. Whether these heroes on great voyages seek fame, fortune or pirate treasure, it's certain that the lure of the ocean and its secrets are as old as time itself.

A resounding theme in ocean folklore is the unknown, and the innate human fear of what one cannot see lurking under the waves in far-flung seas. Many stories tell of ghostly bells, still ringing from the depths of sunken towns that were swallowed by the sea – as if the inhabitants still go about their daily tasks, submerged under the dark waters among the waving seaweed fronds. For many on the biting shores of the Northern Hemisphere the sea is a place of raging storms, ghostly mists and strange noises that pierce the frosty beaches on dark nights – concealing hidden threats to life and land. For those in the southern seas, there are endless tales of sea monsters and temptresses in the exotic waters and sweet lagoons, who lure men to their doom. The very real fear of a fate worse than death itself lingers in the minds of many: that of being a castaway, stranded on a desert island, delirious from thirst, plummeting towards inevitable madness. Tales of shapeshifters are rife throughout the world, as if somewhere, deep within ourselves, we know that the sea cannot be trusted; it morphs and wanes with its ebb and flow, and nothing is ever as it seems. Many sailors have been afflicted by a madness called 'calenture', where, when they stare out to the endless stretch of the ocean waves, they see land instead, and jump over the side to their doom, where they will spend eternity in Davy Jones' Locker on the ocean bed. Another tale is that of ships which finally discovered land, only to realize later that they were in fact resting on a turtle or whale so huge that it resembled a small island rather than any creature of the deep. In more recent times, the new threat of disappearing altogether, with a fate unknown, lingers – especially if sailing close to the North Atlantic's Bermuda Triangle, still a widely debated mystery. Explanations for such disappearances range from tropical cyclones to being carried away by the Gulf Stream, right through to aliens, or to the area being the site of the fabled Atlantis.

When we look at sea folklore from around the world, we find it is often used to explain the unexplainable: unquenchable feelings of lust, illegitimacy, disappearance, bad luck, death, starvation, or a fruitless yield. Folklore indeed teaches us that the sea is dark, illicit and full of temptations. The ocean can offer the things of our wildest dreams – treasure, love, a different life – but to get these we must face our darkest nightmares: the terrifying things that lurk beneath the surface in our subconscious minds. When we face these, and defeat them, we win the treasures of the deep and see sights most can only dream of; yet one thing that folklore teaches – make no mistake – is that the treasures of the sea always come with a price.

Dare you delve further, reach tentatively beneath the dark swell, to see what you might find? Pirate treasures await you, yet take care when your fingers dip into the deep blackness that their tips don't brush against steely scales lurking under the surface. And don't forget: when you do dare to peer below the dancing waves, always listen well for the siren's call …

FAMOUS FLOODS

Some of the most famous flood stories are those of Noah, who makes an appearance in the Christian Bible, Jewish Torah and Islamic Quran. Yet did you know that a devastating flood that almost extinguished humankind is a motif that resounds through myths from all corners of the ancient world? Many nations share a story of a great deluge, and while there are multiple versions of the myth we see common threads running through them all. Many flood myths appear to be tales of the gods' punishment for the errant ways of humans, or for over-population, while others tell of the repopulation of the earth or human origins. One item that appears almost consistently is a boat or vessel that saves a few chosen people as a reward for their piety or wisdom, often filled with all the plants and animals needed to rejuvenate life across the earth. The stories commonly tell of a brother and sister pair, yet some have bewitching details all of their very own, unique to the land where they originate.

We find the roots of Noah's deluge in earlier stories, like that of the ancient Near Eastern *Epic of Gilgamesh*, which was passed down from the Sumerians to the Assyrians and Babylonians. It describes Utnapishtim as a great ancestor who survived a terrible flood and was granted immortality. Utnapishtim was instructed by the god Enki to build a giant boat, called *The Preserver of Life*, on which to keep safe all the animals and plants of the earth, as everything that was not within the ship would be destroyed by a great flood. Afterwards, Utnapishtim sent out three birds: a dove, a sparrow and a raven. Only the raven did not return – a sign that the flood was over. As a reward for his faith, the gods gave him and his wife the gift of immortality.

Many of the Noah stories follow this pattern, yet some have quirky details unique to their country of origin. Noah appears in traditional Indigenous tales of the Dreamtime flood, *woramba*, from the Fitzroy River area of Western Australia, where it's said that the *Ark Gumana* carried Noah, along with Indigenous Australians, finally settling on the flood plain of Djilinbadu. It's believed that the idea of the ark ultimately landing in the Middle East was a lie, to keep Indigenous Australians in subservience. However, another Australian story gives a different explanation for the flood. The medicine man Grumuduk, who could call the rains and cause plants to grow and animals to be fruitful, was kidnapped by a plains tribe. On his escape he vowed that whenever he walked on an enemy's territory, salt water would follow in his path.

Strangely, mice often find themselves in starring roles in the flood myth genre. A Russian folk tale recounts how the Devil told Noah's wife to prepare a strong drink in order to discover Noah's reason for building the ark, which indeed she did, finding out the secret that God had entrusted to him. She was also responsible for the Devil, who had transformed himself into a mouse, secreting himself away on the ark and gnawing holes into the bottom.

An indigenous flood story from northern Siberia also mentions mice. Here, seven people survived the flood on a boat, yet a horrendous drought followed it. They dug a hole, which filled with water, yet all but one man and one woman died from starvation; these two had eaten mice to save themselves. The whole of humankind are descendants of this pair.

The boat is a recurring symbol in many stories. In Hindu tradition, a demon stole the sacred books from Bramha; humanity, in its entirety, became corrupt, apart from the seven Nishis and Satyavrata, the prince of the maritime region. One day, when Satyavrata was bathing, the god Vishnu came to him in the form of a fish, warning him of the great deluge that would come to destroy all that was corrupt on the earth. He told Satyavrata that he would be secured in a capacious vessel, and instructed him to take with him the seven holy men, and fill it with all the plants and animals of the land. With this, Vishnu disappeared, and over the next seven days Satyavrata did as he was commanded and prepared for the waters. Indeed, within a week the rains began. The rivers broke their banks and the oceans flooded the land, bringing a large ship floating towards them. Satyavrata bundled the holy men on board, along with their families, and all the herbs and grains he had been instructed to bring, along with two of each animal. The great Vishnu came again to protect the vessel, by transforming into a giant fish and tying the boat tightly to himself to survive the flood. When the waters subsided, Vishnu killed the demon that had stolen the holy books, and taught their lessons to Satyavrata.

In the flood myth from Cameroon, the prophetic animal is a goat, rather than a fish. The tale tells that a woman was grinding flour one day and allowed a goat to lick it up. In gratitude, the goat warned her to take up her possessions and flee before the flood ensued.

Some flood stories take an even more fantastical turn. For the Soyots of the Republic of Buryatia in Russia the world is carried on the back of a giant frog or turtle. While this idea might be familiar to many, it might surprise you to know that it's told that the creature moved just once and from this tiny act the cosmic ocean flooded the earth; in fact, the creation stories of Eastern Siberia say that if the world frog moves even a little, the world will shake violently, and earthquakes can rain down on humanity.

We also find that many myths link a worldwide flood with giants. Berossus, a Chaldean writer, astronomer and priest of Bel in Babylon in the 3rd century BCE, adds to the Noah story by describing the antediluvians that were left after the flood as a depraved race of giants; all except 'Noa' that is. Instead, Noa revered the gods, and resided in Syria with his three sons: Sem, Jepet and Chem. He foresaw the oncoming destruction in the stars and had set about building a ship to save his family. Remnants of the boat are still said to exist where it settled, on the peak of Gendyae or Mountain, and bitumen was still taken from it to ward off evil well into the 19th century. Similar tales of an antediluvian race of giants exist in Scandinavian flood traditions, where Odin, Vili and Ve defeated the primordial giant Ymir. All but two of the giants, Bergelmir and his wife, were killed in a great flood that arose from the blood of Ymir's gushing wounds. All giants are descended from these two.

Stranger still, elves appear in a Chingpaw flood story from the northern region of Myanmar. In this tale, brother and sister Pawpaw Nan-chaung and Chang-hko fled to safety on a boat, taking nine cocks and nine needles with them. Once the rain had ceased, they threw one of each from the boat, until they came to the last pair. On throwing these overboard, they finally heard the cock crow and the sound of the needle hitting the bottom. With this they were able to return to dry land, and soon came upon a cave in which two elves had made their home. The siblings stayed with the elves in their cave, and all was well with them; that is until Chang-hko gave birth, and left the infant in the care of the elfin woman while she went out to work. This is where the story takes a gruesome turn: the woman was a witch! Faced with the incessant wailing of the child, the witch took it to a crossroads where nine roads met, chopped it to pieces and scattered the body about, yet keeping a little with her, with nefarious intent. On her return to the cave, the elf-witch made a curry from the remaining parts of the babe, feeding it to the unsuspecting mother. When she discovered the truth, in her utter dismay, Chang-hko fled to the crossroads to plead with the Great Spirit to avenge her child and bring it back to life. The Great Spirit deemed this impossible, but instead promised to transform the remaining pieces of her child into the next generations of humankind – one branch for each of the nine paths – making her the mother of all nations to ease her pain.

MERMAIDS, SELKIES AND SIRENS

The folklore of the sea is filled with tales of half-human hybrids; these creatures, often exceedingly beautiful in either looks or voice, exact a strong allure over those they come into contact with. Whether beguiling with their beauty or with the exquisite nature of their singing, these creatures can be both benign and terrifying, helping humans if it serves their purpose, or luring them to a wet and watery end if the mood takes them.

While there are similarities between the mermaids, selkies and sirens that fill the lore of the sea, there are telling differences, as we will discover below.

Seductress or Saviour? The Timeless Lure of the Mermaid

Tales of mermaids have frequented folklore, children's literature and popular culture in recent times. The origins of these long long-haired, fish-tailed, half-human beauties, however, stretch back surprisingly far into history.

An Assyrian myth from 1000BCE tells of Atargatis, a beautiful fertility goddess. One of the many tellings of her story describes how she fell in love with a handsome young man, but tragedy was not far behind. Some say he was unable to keep up with her love-making, while other versions of the tale say that it was the birth of her human child that caused her great shame. Whatever the cause, the outcome was the same: Atargatis killed her lover and, unable to stand the guilt, she threw herself into the sea. Her desire was to become a fish in penance for her terrible actions, but it was not to be. Her beauty meant that the transformation could only be half-complete, and the grieving goddess found herself with her old human head and body but, below the waist, with the tail of a fish.

From then onwards, mermaids have become a staple of popular culture and belief, spreading throughout the world in numerous forms and incarnations. Some mermaids were said to have shown kindness towards humans. The mermaid encountered by an old man in Cury, Cornwall, rewarded his lack of greed by granting him many mysterious powers and bequeathing a magic comb that was passed down through the generations of his family. More often than not, however, mermaids receive bad press and their relationships with humans are reported as decidedly negative; for instance, the Brazilian Iara or Yara is known for tempting sailors down to her palace under the waves for a watery end.

Christopher Columbus famously recorded a sighting during a voyage in 1493, declaring the 'mermaids' he had witnessed as: 'Not half as beautiful as they are painted.' This scathing assessment might be explained scientifically; it has since been thought that what he had actually seen were manatees, sea cows or dugongs.

Perhaps the best-known and most well-loved mermaid is Hans Christian Andersen's *The Little Mermaid*, a story inspired by earlier mermaid folk tales, in which the famous storyteller used fairy-tale tropes to conjure a magical narrative beloved by many today. Written in 1836 and published the following year, Andersen's mermaid has been represented in dozens of incarnations and variations over the almost two centuries since she first appeared on the printed page. Often reimagined and retold for modern audiences, the tale is one of many now at the centre of debates about gender, sexuality and feminism in folk tales and literary fairy tales. The mermaid is commemorated today by a statue that rests at Langelinie, Copenhagen, Denmark; fashioned out of bronze, she is a copy of the original designed by Edward Eriksen and erected in 1913.

The Little Mermaid: A Tale from Denmark

Once there was a mermaid, the youngest of six princesses, who lived in a beautiful kingdom beneath the sea. Her mother was dead, but her father, the Merman King, ruled with the support of their grandmother from a breathtaking palace made of coral and amber and a mussel-shell roof. Although the youngest of the sisters, the mermaid was the most beautiful of them all, famed for her soft skin and deep blue eyes. She was of a contemplative nature, calm and content.

Each of the princesses had a small garden, and while the others filled theirs with all manner of beautiful things, the youngest mermaid had nothing in hers but flowers that were like the sun and a marble statue of a beautiful boy. For the young mermaid was greatly taken with the human world above, begging for tales from anyone who might know anything of what went on there. Such stories only increased her fascination, and the little mermaid longed to see it for herself. This was not a forlorn hope; when each princess reached the age of 15 they were permitted to rise up above the waves and sit on the rocks by night, to watch the ships and experience a little of the world of humankind.

One by one her sisters had their turn, and the youngest mermaid watched and waited and listened to their experiences, each passing year only increasing her desire and longing to see for herself. Finally, when she felt she could wait no longer, her turn came. Sunset had just passed when the little mermaid rose up through the ocean for the first time, to find a calm sea and golden streaks fading in the sky. Drinking in the fascinating sights, the sound of a party in full swing on a nearby ship caught her attention; captivated, she swam closer for a better look.

There were many people celebrating, but the one who caught her eye was a young prince; it was his birthday, and he was the most handsome sight the mermaid had ever seen. She watched and watched, enjoying the brightly coloured rockets that were set off in his honour, the lights and flashes and gaiety little short of magic in her eyes. The mermaid could not tear herself away even after the last strains of music had long faded, the ship now in darkness as the night went on. So she was there to witness the sudden breaking of the calm: an unexpected storm rolling in, shattering the peace of the night. Waves crashed higher and higher, rolling over the deck, the ship at the mercy of the tempest.

As the little mermaid looked on, the main mast was snapped like a piece of kindling, the helpless vessel tossed onto its side as those onboard flailed desperately in the water. Despite great danger from floating debris, the little mermaid found the prince, holding his head out of the water and keeping him safe as the storm finally died down. As dawn broke she took her precious prize to the nearest land, setting him on the beach carefully before retreating to watch. Before long, the prince was discovered by a young woman, who ran for help, and the mermaid watched sadly from behind a rock as he was carried off to warmth and safety.

The mermaid returned to her home but could not forget the prince; growing increasingly quiet and withdrawn, she pined for the young man and the world she had left him to. When she admitted the cause of her sadness to a sister word soon spread, and it was revealed that the location of the prince's kingdom was known to another mermaid. The princesses took their sister there, and the little mermaid now spent her evenings near the palace, watching what went on there and waiting for glimpses of her prince. Instead of soothing her troubled heart, more and more she wished for an immortal soul like humans possessed; alas, being a mermaid, this was not to be. Instead, like any mermaid, she was destined to spend 300 years beneath the waves, before her form would be dissolved into foam.

Was there nothing she could do to gain a soul? she asked her grandmother one day in despair. There was only one thing, the

old woman told her in return: if a mortal man loved her more than anything in the world and married her, her body would then become infused with his soul and she would achieve her wish. It could not be, however, for she had only a tail – and how could a mortal man love someone who is half fish?

Far from being dissuaded, and with her grandmother's words fresh in her mind, that night the mermaid decided to seek help elsewhere. There was a terrible sea witch known for her great powers, and the mermaid set off to ask for her advice. The journey was terrifying and hard, through bare grey sands and bubbling mud, with trees and bushes that were alive, grabbing and pulling at those unwary enough to get too close. Horrified, the mermaid saw in the mud the bones of animals and humans who had drowned. It was so tempting to turn back and return to her lovely home, but the determined little mermaid continued on her way.

Finally she reached the house of the sea witch, who already knew the reason for her visit. It was foolishness, declared the witch, but if she was determined to go through with it, there was a way that it could be done. To swap her tail for human legs and have the chance to gain an immortal soul and be with her prince, the witch would make her a potion; before sunrise came she must swim ashore, sit on the beach and drink it. Her tail would then divide and shrivel, becoming instead the two legs she so coveted. It would come at a price, however, the witch warned. The process would be painful and feel like she was being run through with a sword. Not only that, every step the mermaid took on her new feet would feel like treading upon knives as she went. She would, however, without doubt, be the most beautiful girl the kingdom had ever seen.

A more faint-hearted girl might have balked at this, but the mermaid stood firm and agreed, her love for the prince so great she was willing to suffer anything to have the chance to win his heart. She would not be able to reverse the process, the witch warned: she would never be a mermaid again and would therefore never see her family under the waves. Also, if she didn't manage to convince the prince to love her, she would not gain a soul, and on the first morning after his marriage to someone else her heart would break before she instantly turned into foam in the sea. Even to these terrible conditions the mermaid agreed, but there was yet more. As payment, the sea witch demanded the girl's beautiful voice in the form of her tongue. Again the little mermaid did not hesitate, and her tongue was duly cut out, the witch making the promised potion for her.

Grief-stricken at the thought of not seeing her family again, but hopeful for what was to come, the mermaid made her way to the beach. Drinking the potion down she felt the first stab of agony course through her as the witch had promised. It did not matter, however, as the prince himself appeared at that moment and, as she looked at herself, the mermaid gleefully saw that her tail was gone, human legs now in their place.

Intrigued, the prince asked her name, but of course she could not tell him that or anything else about herself. Instead, she was taken to the palace, where she was given clothes and looked after as a valued guest. The prince became very fond of the little mermaid, and the pair were inseparable. She slept on a velvet cushion outside his room, and he took her riding with him, climbed mountains as they explored the kingdom, and she smiled and looked on him with love even as her feet bled. The prince did love her in return, but, alas, as a child, not as a future wife, and the proposal of marriage she so longed for and needed never came. For the prince confided in his silent confidante that he was in love with the girl who had discovered him on the beach after the fateful storm, and he could now love no other. This news nearly broke the mermaid's heart, especially as without her tongue she could not tell him that it was she who had saved his life that night, and was powerless to reveal her identity.

As time went on, rumours started to circulate that a bride had been chosen for the prince. Yet the mermaid did not worry, as he had told her that because there was only one girl for him he would never wed. To keep up the pretence, however, he made the voyage to where his prospective wife lived in a neighbouring kingdom; the mermaid – his constant attendant – accompanied him on the journey. In a terrible stroke of fate for the mermaid, it turned out that the princess was the very same girl who had helped save the prince; overjoyed, the prince at once consented to marry her and preparations for a grand wedding were soon underway. The mermaid played her part with smiles and all signs of happiness, even as her feet bled and the pain in her heart grew ever greater as she knew that this marriage would bring with it her death.

One night, the mermaid received a visit from her sisters. They were barely recognizable as their hair was shorn off; out of love for the little mermaid they had made a bargain with the sea witch, swapping their hair for a knife that would save their sister's life. She had only to stab the prince with it when he slept and the spell would be reversed; the little mermaid could then return to her 300 years as a mermaid and an end dissolving in the foam.

The mermaid took the knife and crept into the room where the prince slept, a smile on his lips as he dreamed of his new bride. Gazing down at him, she felt her heart almost burst with love, and in that moment she knew she could not carry out her task. With a final look at him she turned and left, throwing the knife far out into the sea. A moment later the mermaid followed, throwing herself into the deep water, where she dissolved into foam.

Despite the witch's dire prediction, however, all was not over for the little mermaid. She was greeted by the daughters of the air, spirits who had been offered the chance to strive for 300 years doing good deeds in order to earn an immortal soul. If they were successful, they would reach heaven, and the little mermaid, through her suffering and selflessness, would now have the chance to do the same. Gladly, she accepted the offer, bidding farewell to the earth and sea below as she rose up into the clouds above.

THE KING OF HUMBUG: P.T. BARNUM AND THE FEEJEE MERMAID

Being elusive creatures, it isn't often that the opportunity arises to see a mermaid in the flesh. In 1842, however, visitors to New York were presented with just such a chance, when the now infamous Feejee Mermaid went on show at Barnum's American Museum, through the connivance of arch-hoaxer P.T. Barnum. Believed to be of Japanese origin, the 'mermaid' – measuring an estimated 45–90cm (11/2–3ft) long – was actually the desiccated body of a monkey sewn to the back half of a fish. Despite disappointment expressed by some visitors, the exhibit was a hit, with Barnum's profits doubling in the first month the 'mermaid' was on show.

Not long afterwards, the mermaid mysteriously vanished; some stories say it perished in a fire, while others are convinced that, against all odds, it escaped this ignoble fate. Is a similar mermaid in the possession of the Peabody Museum at Harvard University in fact the original Feejee Mermaid?

The Call of the Siren

Perhaps most famous for their failure to claim Odysseus in Homer's *Odyssey*, the sirens have long held a place in the folklore of the sea. These aptly named 'entanglers' were thought to be of great peril to seamen: their aim was to lure the unwary onto the rocks (using only the irresistible beauty of their singing), where their victims were dashed to pieces. Others who encountered the sirens simply forgot everything save for the attraction of their voices, eschewing food and drink until they likewise perished.

Although often linked with mermaids, the appearance of the sirens differs in one crucial way: while a mermaid is a woman/fish hybrid, the siren was described as half-woman, half-bird. They were also not originally portrayed as creatures of great beauty: it was their voices that stood out rather than their physical appearance, the sweet notes knowing no rival and proving so deadly irresistible. Over time, however, this focus has subtly shifted, and in later depictions – such as John William Waterhouse's painting *The Siren* (c.1900) – their physical charms have increased to match those of their voices.

In the classical sources, the number of sirens varies: Homer mentions two, whereas as many as five have been reported, with varying names and locations. The origin of these golden-voiced temptresses is also hazy, and the sirens are named as daughters of varying deities, including the Greek sea god Phorcys or the river god Achelous. Where most sources agree, however, is that the sirens were cold and calculating, almost universally considered to be negative beings. Biblically, in the Apocrypha, women and angels who go astray are condemned to become sirens on the Day of Judgement. In the *Septuagint* translation of the Hebrew Bible into Greek, Na'amah is equated with sirens and the term is mentioned in several places throughout.

Unsurprisingly given their favoured pastime, the sirens and the folklore surrounding them have an enduring link with death. Ovid names them as companions to Persephone in her time in the Underworld, and the Siren of Canosa – of which a terracotta figure showing a woman with the feet, tail and wings of a bird can be seen in the National Archaeological Museum in Madrid – is believed to have been sent with the dead among their grave goods to the afterlife.

The Selkie-folk, the Shapeshifting Seals of the Northern Seas

For those that live on the shores of the icy waters of Orkney and Shetland, the raging waves and skerries provide an atmospheric backdrop to tales of the selkie-folk. While originally dark, malevolent creatures, selkies later became renowned as beautiful and gentle, often found dancing on the sand under moonlit skies. Selkies emerge from the waves as seals, only shedding their magical skin when they reach the shore, transforming into human form as they cast it away. Many tales tell that if the skin is taken and hidden the selkie cannot return to the sea to live with their selkie-kin, and must stay in human form until it is returned.

One such folk tale is remembered in a famous Orcadian ballad, 'The Great Silkie of Sule Skerry'. In this tragic tale, an Orkney maiden falls in love with a selkie man, who abandons her shortly after she gives birth to their child. Seven years later, a seal appears to her and tells her that he is her lover, only to dive once more into the sea. Another seven years pass, and the seal appears once more. This time he gives the gift of a golden chain to their son, who goes with him to live in the sea. The woman remarries, and many years later her husband is out hunting one day and shoots two seals. On returning to the house, he gives his wife the gold chain that he found around the neck of the younger seal. She realizes that her husband has tragically killed both her son and selkie lover.

Male selkies were often blamed for the disappearance of young women who wandered too close to the seashore alone at night. Many disappearances were put down to the girls being whisked away and taken as lovers by selkie men, who easily conquered the mortal women with their seductive powers. Indeed, women used to paint crosses on their daughter's breasts to ward off the selkie-folk when they set out on a journey across the sea, yet a selkie lover was often coveted.

Selkie nymphs were said to have snow-white skin and large, dark eyes, and be just as irresistible as the males. Old stories say that they often sat on rocks in groups, basking in the sun, and if disturbed they would hurriedly slip back into their skins and swim away. 'The Goodman of Wastness' tells of a man who refused to marry a woman of his own kind, but set about stealing the skin of one unfortunate sea-maiden after stumbling upon a group of them one day. The selkies leapt into the sea and swam away, yet all but one had donned their skins and returned to their seal form. As he bundled her skin away and turned to leave, he heard the maiden weeping, begging him to give back what he had stolen. At her pleading he instantly fell in love with her, and implored her to stay with him as his wife. She agreed, but only because she couldn't return to the sea without her skin, which he refused to return. As the years passed the couple had seven children and were content. Yet each time the man left the house his wife would search high and low for the skin that was stolen from her on that fateful day long ago. One day, when she was searching as usual, her daughter asked her what she was looking for, to which she replied, 'A skin to make shoes from,' to help her daughter's injured foot. The daughter said she had seen her father take out the skin a time ago, when he thought her to be asleep. The selkie wife rushed to the place, pulled out the skin and ran to the beach. And, slipping it on, she leapt into the sea to return to her selkie husband.

Many children on the Orkney Isles have been said to have 'selkiepaws' – webbing between their fingers and toes. For instance, there are accounts of a 19th-century midwife who attributed this to their selkie parentage, and repeatedly cut it away to prevent fins forming from their tiny hands.

TO SUMMMON A SELKIE LOVER

Many folk have yearned to meet a selkie lover over the years, and when the secret method of calling one to you was uncovered, it was passed down from generation to generation as prized knowledge, as it is now passed on to you here. First, you should wait until the perfect time to meet your lover, this of course being high tide. When this time has come, you must go quickly to the ocean waves. Once you have reached the shore, you should shed seven tears into the sea – no more, and no fewer. At this, a potential selkie lover will appear in front of you in the waves. But be warned: sadness follows many who take a selkie as their life-partner, as most will always yearn for the waves until their days are done.

From Mermaid to Serpent Queen: The Many Guises of Mami Wata

Mystical, ever-changing, many things to many people; the African water deity known as Mami Wata is a complex and multifaceted spirit. Most popularly depicted as half-woman, half-fish, with long, wavy black hair, her likeness to the popular and seductive mermaid of legend and folklore is immediately inescapable, highlighting the hybrid and shifting nature of folklore between different times and continents. Her nature is like that of the sea itself: powerful, changeable, alluring, both willing to give, and to take away. She is worshipped throughout West, Central and Southern Africa, as well as within the African diasporas: throughout the Caribbean, Latin America and the USA.

Her origins are often debated, but it is generally accepted that Mami Wata is not indigenous to the African countries that have become her home over the centuries. With a long tradition of part water creature, part human deities in such areas, however, it is unsurprising that she has thrived and taken root there.

The primordial water spirit, noted for her overwhelming beauty, Tingoi (or Njaloi) has been identified as a precursor to Mami Wata, and forms the link between sea, water deity and serpent. Sometimes depicted as a mix of serpent and fish, Tingoi has the head of a human woman, long, black locks of hair and a stunning appearance, not to mention the powerful lure she holds over those who follow her, heavily suggestive of later mermaids of European lore and Mami Wata herself. Receptiveness to such beings was already present when, in the 15th century, through contact made from trade and conquest, the mermaid was taken by African peoples and reimagined, emerging as the fully African Mami Wata.

Another link between Mami Wata and mermaid lore is through the connection both have to mirrors. The image of a mermaid combing her luxurious locks while admiring her reflection is a common one, and Mami Wata is likewise often depicted with her own treasured glass. Mirrors are also used by her followers to make contact with Mami Wata; they form an important piece of Mami Wata worship and identification and are present at her shrines. Mirrors represent the reflective surface of the water, but also allude to her ability to transgress boundaries. They are said to attract her to them because of her vanity, drawing her presence to wherever she is needed. Her devotees mirror her in their worship: recreating her underwater realms within their sacred spaces, impersonating her in rituals, and even entering possession trance states to gain her favour. However similar some of her traits may seem to mermaid traditions, though, the worship of Mami Wata is very much a living belief, one that has been called a 'uniquely African faith' that developed in times of trade with the wider world.

In possession of many powers, Mami Wata is generous and bountiful, bestowing them upon those who follow her, well-known for bringing wealth and fortune to those she favours. Fertility is also said to be in her boon, despite her own infertile and childless state. Another power possessed by this deity is that of healing, in both body and mind. It is said that the most favoured of her followers have sometimes been taken down to her watery realm beneath the sea, returning to their life on dry land changed beyond recognition forever.

Despite her great power for good, there is a darker side to Mami Wata. While giving gifts in one moment, in the next she can and will take them away, striking with sudden wrath those who displease her. Illness, suffering beyond measure, even death itself is said to come at her hand. There is also said to be a limit to her bounty; to those she grants wealth, beauty is beyond their grasp, and those upon whom she bestows fertility, wealth will never be theirs. Mami Wata is a powerful female, nurturing and sexual potency fully co-existing within this most complex

of deities. Yet she is also prone to jealousy, demanding faithful celibacy from men in Zaire in return for wealth, and it's said in Ghana that she can even kill a man's wife. For the Igbo of Nigeria, Mami Wata can also punish with illness, especially if feeling slighted at not receiving enough attention from her followers.

Although unpredictable, one of the many lures of Mami Wata is the very fluidity of her nature. The Krio of Sierra Leone look to the Moa River as the source of all life; the river is wild and unpredictable, mirroring the nature of Mami Wata who lives within it. Capable of morphing and being formed into whatever is needed by each individual person who calls on her, Mami Wata's appeal is that she can be many things to many different people at any given time. Her shifting and hybrid nature is illustrated in a physical sense in an Efik sculpture of Mami Wata, where she is represented as a mixture of woman, goat and fish, while in her hands she holds a snake and a bird. In some locations, Mami Wata is found in a plural form, as mami watas, and even in male form as papi watas.

Mami Wata has enjoyed a resurgence in attention in recent years, and there has been a general increase in interest in African deities. Such interest in Mami Wata in particular has also been spurred on by popular singer Beyoncé's fascination with the deity and allusions to Mami Wata in her album *Lemonade* and her own personal depiction of the goddess. An exhibition examining Mami Wata was held at UCLA in 2008, while the MAMI exhibition of 2016, held at the Knockdown Centre, New York, examined the different ways six women-identifying artists related to and identified with Mami Wata.

Some suggest that there is a less positive facet of Mami Wata: that far from empowering women of colour, the idolization of the spirit is actually harmful, reinforcing the derogatory image of black women as 'manipulative eye candy'. Largely, however, her reception is seen as a positive thing, capturing the imagination of and empowering many as the powerful water goddess is reinvented afresh for a modern audience.

THE FABLED COAST OF PUGLIA

Locals of the Puglia region of Italy – nestled in the heel of the boot – will tell you there is a great rivalry about which sea is the best: the wild Ionian of the west coast of the peninsula, or the bright turquoise Adriatic of the east. Whichever side you come down on, the legends of both are equally captivating.

The Adriatic is filled with mystery; it sparkles with promise under the heat of the sun as bathers cool themselves, and we can only wonder what treasures the depths hold. It is a sea that has captured our imaginations for thousands of years, yet its magic has never diminished: it is a place filled with sea stacks and grottoes peppered along the coastal cliffs.

The Legend of Cristalda and Pizzomunno

One folk tale from the region is so tragically beautiful that it captures hearts still, and in 2018 the leading Italian artist Max Gazzè released a single for the 68th Sanremo Music Festival based on the age-old Pugliese love story, 'La Leggenda Di Cristalda e Pizzomunno', which some say dates back to the 15th century. The tale is set against the clear blue waters of Vieste – a seaside village in the province of Foggia on the Adriatic coast – known as the Pearl of the Gargano. From the clifftops you can look down over Castello beach and see the stark white form of the Pizzomunno sea stack breaking through the waters and reaching up to touch the sky.

Those sailing in the waters nearby whisper rumours that the rock sometimes disappears in the dead of night – with no reasonable explanation. Others say that a wish will come true if spoken while circling the sea stack. The folk tale itself tells of Pizzomunno, a brave young fisherman of Vieste. While many girls coveted his attentions, the fisherman had eyes for nothing and nobody – except the lure of the sea itself, and one woman alone: Cristalda, the most beautiful of all. The village girls were envious of their love, watching night after night as the pair embraced on the shore, or walked arm in arm. Yet these girls were not the only danger the pair faced. Each day, when Pizzomunno took his ship out to sea, the evil faces of wayward sirens would call out to him, their ethereal voices from beneath the waves trying to lure him into the depths to live in their fairy-tale kingdom with promises of devotion. Yet, day after day, Pizzomunno remained true to his love.

One night, Pizzomunno and Cristalda sat on the shore as always, under the watchful gaze of the sirens. In the days that followed, the sirens' songs became even more bewitching. Still, day after day, Pizzomunno remained true, until the sirens resorted to threats. Pizzomunno only laughed at them, proclaiming he would love Cristalda forever – even after his death.

And here the tale turns into one that teaches the fate of those who dare to mock the sirens: for their wrath is famous throughout all the lands of the earth. And this wrath fell heavily upon the young couple's shoulders, for the sirens decreed that Pizzomunno must be punished for his mockery and ability to resist their temptations, and this love – purer than any other – must come to an end. And so it did. For soon, as the lovers lay under the watchful stars of the warm Mediterranean skies, the sirens launched their frenzied attack. Grabbing at Cristalda, the sirens quickly bound her with chains and dragged her down to the depths of the sea.

Pizzomunno, of course, gave chase, flinging himself into the water after Cristalda and her captors, yet to no avail. Soon

the fisherman was exhausted with his efforts, and – losing all hope – he slowly turned to stone in his grief. Yet, unbeknown to Pizzomunno in his petrified state, Cristalda watched on over his plight from the sirens' fairy-tale realm, plunged into her own grief at the fate of her love. Unable to bear this torment, it's said that she too transformed: becoming as cold as ice, she began to change into a pillar of pink coral, from which tears fall to this day like pearls, still chained to the underwater vault in the realm of the sirens.

Yet all was not lost, for the tale tells of one final hope for the lovers. Every 100 years they are able to take back their human forms for just one night, and embrace once more on the flat rock that lies in the bay of Vieste, hand in hand, before returning to the sea once more. And there they stand, the stone stack of Pizzomunno rising up from the ebbing waves, looking down on his Cristalda in her pink coral form under the sea, as they wait for the sands of another century to trickle by.

Some, it's said, have an answer for the questioning sailors that now sail Vieste's coast, at least on the night of 15 August if no other. For if, on this night specifically, the Pizzomunno rock cannot be seen from the waters, then the man himself can be found on shore in the embrace of his one true love, Cristalda.

The Dolphin of Taranto

Across the peninsula – close to the arid squares of Taranto – the clear blue waves of the Ionian Sea lap at the Lungomare di Taranto, the Gulf of Taranto coast.

Taranto itself is most well-known for its famous *pizzica tarantata* dance, dating back to the 14th century, where participants convulse on the ground in a frenzy accompanied by tambourines. This is a healing ritual against the bite of the wolf spider, known locally as the *tarantula*, which many erroneously believed to be poisonous, causing a condition called 'tarantism', in essence a state of hysterics similar to dancing mania. The ritual dance is performed to neutralize the poison by exorcizing the demon through the will of St Paul, the patron saint of sufferers. An 18th-century remedy advises that the tongue of a petrified snake should be placed in wine, which is then drunk by the sufferer after the ninth dance, as there are three dances a day for three days.

The Gulf of Taranto coast is also filled with legends. Once described by 2nd-century Greek traveller Pausanias as the largest and most prosperous city on the coast, Taranto itself has many origin stories. While some tales tell that the city was named after Taras, the son of the ancient sea god Poseidon and a local nymph, another tells that it was founded by Taras himself. The legend states that when Taras was shipwrecked near the coast of Taranto, Poseidon sent a dolphin to save his son. Taras rode this creature to the shore, where the city was founded in honour of the god's merciful act. Many ancient coins from the area show a man – identified as Taras by scholars like Aristotle – riding on a dolphin, often with Poseidon's trident in his hand. This is still the emblem of the city today. Interestingly, in 2016, a Taranto-based shoe company, Sneakers76, worked with Puma to create a pair of trainers named 'The Legend of the Dolphin' to celebrate the company's tenth anniversary. In honour of the origin story of their home town, the colour scheme was chosen to represent the blue waves and grey dolphin, with brown laces alluding to the bridle used by Taras to ride it. It's wonderful to see how deeply the legend pervades the minds of the city's people to this day, with pride in their cultural identity displayed even in the fashions they design and wear.

In contrast to the beauty of the rest of the Salento region, Taranto is now often called the Red City. Yet its pink-hued, candyfloss skies exist for a sinister reason: environmental disaster. Reports claim that pollution from the largest steel plant in Europe, in the form of toxic dust, is causing cancer-related deaths in the area. Supported by the European Court of Justice, locals have campaigned for years to reclaim the clean air that their forebearers would have known, to match the clear crystal-blue waters of legend.

The Priestess Io and the Ionian Sea

The history of the Ionian Sea that Taranto sits upon is one of a woman scorned. Myth tells that when Zeus saw the priestess Io he was overcome with lust, intent on taking her for his own, as the old gods often did. Hera, ever watchful of her philandering husband, was consumed with suspicion. Covering his tracks quickly, Zeus transformed Io into a white heifer to conceal his dastardly deed. Yet Hera, knowing her husband too well, cleverly asked to be given the cow as a gift. With more than cunning on her side, Hera commanded that Io be tied to an olive tree at Nemea, and tasked the giant Argus the All-seeing to watch over the heifer with his numerous unsleeping eyes. Yet, not to be outdone in his quest for a lusty rendezvous, Zeus's son Hermes charmed the giant to sleep at his father's request, removed his eyes, and promptly killed him. At this Io fled, crossing over the sea which then took her name. Though chased by a gadfly under Hera's command, Io managed to reach Egypt, where she took her rightful form, and gave birth to a son. In honour of his service, Hera took each of Argus' eyes – rumoured to number 100 – and placed them forevermore in the peacock's tail.

MONSTERS FROM THE DEEP

Tales of monstrous sea creatures span the centuries, appearing as early as the dawn of writing itself. Many sea serpents embody creation and primordial chaos, and can be found in end-times myths from across the globe – stories that tell of the end of the world. Tiamat is one of the first, described in ancient Mesopotamian tablets known as the *Enûma Eliš*. Seen as a great dragon, she is sometimes a creator goddess, while a symbol of primordial chaos for others – a thing that has filled humankind with dread since the earliest times. The myth tells of the joining of Tiamat, the personification of the saltwater ocean, with Apsu, the god of the fresh water. These two ruled together at the dawn of time, and were primeval waters in the cosmic abyss. Younger gods were born from this union, living within the body of the great Tiamat and making a great noise, which angered Apsu, hence he planned their demise. When the younger gods found out about his intentions, Marduk and Enki killed Apsu in revenge, and a great battle between the gods ensued, ending with Tiamat's death – a symbol of the new gods overcoming the watery chaos that existed at the beginning of time. Marduk created the heavens and the earth from the two halves of Tiamat's body on her death, and created people as slaves to the gods from the blood of her lover-son, Kingu.

According to Jewish tradition, the fearless Leviathan of the *Talmud Baba Bathra* is said to be a multiple-headed sea serpent or crocodile, which emits a noxious gas from his mouth that makes the waters boil like an apothecary's mixture. Breathing fire, his scales are his pride and his teeth are terrible. What many people haven't heard of is his female counterpart; it was said that if the two mated the world would be destroyed, so the female was salted and preserved to be fed to the righteous at a glorious banquet on the Day of Judgement. Tasty!

Tales of primordial snakes and serpents come from many mythologies. Jörmungandr, the Midgard Serpent of Norse mythology, is one of the children of Loki along with Hel and Fenris-Wolf. He was thrown into the sea that encircles Midgard by the gods because of a prophecy that great misfortune would befall them due to Loki's offspring. At this, he grew so large that his body now encircles the entire visible world and he can grasp the end of his own tail with his maw. As sworn enemies, Thor is destined to slay Jörmungandr when Ragnarök – the battle at the end of the world – arrives.

Surprisingly, giant squid are not in fact mythical sea monsters at all, despite growing to the length of a school bus; the largest ever found measured close to a colossal 18m (nearly 60ft). One legendary creature often depicted as a terrifying giant squid is the Kraken, a sea monster hailing from Scandinavia. Erik Pontoppidan, an 18th-century historian, describes the Kraken as 'round, flat, and full of arms, or branches', with a back 2.5km (1.5 miles) in circumference. It's said to resemble a series of small islands at first, with something floating around that looks like seaweed, and then, finally, huge tentacles as tall as a mast appear from the depths. The only way to escape his fearsome clutches is to row away before he surfaces, and then lie on your oars for safety. Apparently, fishermen have always been glad to find him, as his presence leads to an abundance of fish – yet the fishermen never stay in his vicinity for long, as even his retreat back into the sea causes whirlpools that will drag anything close down into the depths forever.

Sea monsters still capture our imagination today. A 1920s hoax told that a sea monster was to blame for the sinking of a German submarine in 1918, when Captain Günther Krech's vessel,

UB-85, was damaged by a strange beast with 'horns, deep-set eyes and glinting teeth'. A contender for the wreck was found in 2016, yet historians from Bournemouth University said tales of sea monsters and the sinking of U-boats grew from the secrecy that surrounded precisely what took place during the first U-boat battles. Stories often arose as a result of journalists and ex-Navy men 'talking late at night, after having a nice time'. Sea monsters appear in contemporary culture, for instance the terrifying sea serpents of Robin Hobb's *Liveship Traders* trilogy (1998–2000), or the fearsome Kraken in *Pirates of the Caribbean: Dead Man's Chest* (2006), yet some reject all claims of their existence. Many dismiss them as mere oarfish turned legend, often citing the example that washed up on the shore of a Bermuda beach in 1860 – initially called a sea serpent – as evidence. Yet sea monsters linger on in our imagination, maybe as they are often perceived as spiritual symbols of the subconscious mind and our hidden fears, quietly lurking deep in our nightmares to this day.

Scylla and Charybdis

We've all heard people say they're stuck 'between Scylla and Charybdis', but do you know there's more to the phrase than just being 'between a rock and a hard place'? In Greek mythology, Scylla was a terrifying monster that lurked in a cave on the Calabrian side of the Strait of Messina in southern Italy, while Charybdis lived on the Sicilian side.

Tales tell that Charybdis was a feared whirlpool that vomited ships and drowned seafarers by sucking water down to the depths of the abyss, then hurling them back up, 'lashing the stars with waves'.

Scylla was said to be a creature with a human face, with the tails of dolphins, while her nether regions were surrounded by the heads of ravenous dogs – yet this wasn't always so. Hers is a woeful tale of a beautiful virgin and a lover scorned. On being pursued by Glaucus, an unrelenting suitor, she was horrified to see his tail, making her question whether he was a god or a monster. Glaucus explained that he was certainly an equal of the watery gods. When sorting his catch in a field after fishing one day, he saw the fish eating the grass and then miraculously returning to the sea. On seeing this wonder he too ate a little and was then compelled to plunge into the waves forever. The gentle powers of the ocean took him as their brother, and prayed to Tethys to purge his mortal, earthly parts away by repeatedly reading a secret charm. Glaucus bathed in 100 streams, and became of the sea for evermore: falling into dark oblivion, he woke with a sea-green beard, azure skin and a fishy tail. At this story, Scylla scorned his love and fled. Glaucus went to the monstrous realms of the sorceress Circe to plead for one of her baneful love potions that would ensure that Scylla should feel the same agonies of love as he did. Hearing this, Circe revealed her own desires for him, and when rejected, vowed her revenge. Circe went to the cave where

Scylla had sought shelter and poisoned the water there. Scylla was transformed into a monster forever, as her destiny decreed.

From that day hence, Scylla has plucked sailors from any passing ship that drew near to her to avoid the dreaded Charybdis, devouring them alive as the screams of her 'dark blue ocean hounds' echo from the cave walls. Indeed, Odysseus himself had to navigate between the two monsters, and was advised by Circe to sail closer to Scylla, or risk losing his entire ship to Charybdis. He took her advice and only six of his crew died – one apiece eaten raw by each of Scylla's heads. Many have rationalized Scylla as the treacherous rocks of the Italian coast, which do indeed devour wayward ships.

ISLANDS OF FABLE AND MYTH

With the sea featuring prominently in the lives and cultures of so much of the world, it is hardly surprising to discover an underlying fascination with tales of mysterious islands among the legends that pass down to us. Some of these are purely fictional in their creation, while others are linked to either a former or existing geographical location, ready to be discovered by an intrepid folklore explorer. Beware of such a quest, however: these islands prove notoriously elusive to those who wish to find them. Variously invisible, difficult to locate due to shifting position and generally hard to pin down, they remain a tantalizing focus for adventurer and myth-lover alike.

In Slavic folklore, the island of Buyan is home to several fascinating characters and tales. The north, east and west winds are said to live there: indeed, weather of every type is said to originate from Buyan. The island is also known as the place where the sun both rises and sets each day, with two goddesses, the morning star and evening star, helping the sun on its way and welcoming it back each night.

Koschei, known as 'the deathless', is closely linked with Buyan, as the island was the secret location where he hid his soul. Certain that the only way to cheat death was to keep his soul and body separate, Koschei took no chances. His soul was said to have been concealed with ever-increasing intricacy: in some tellings it was to be found within a needle, within an egg, within a duck. Despite his best efforts, Koschei could not avoid his fate forever, and there are several versions of how he finally met his end. In one he was killed by a blow from a small stone hidden in the yolk of an egg – which in turn was hidden inside a hare, itself inside a duck.

Another slight variation on the egg theme is less complicated: Koschei dies when he is hit on the forehead by the egg in question. A further version tells how Prince Ivan breaks the egg containing Koschei's soul, thereby causing his death.

Buyan is also said to be the location of alatuir, a mythical stone attributed with many magical properties. The most powerful of all stones, various sources describe alatuir as protecting a river of healing that flows beneath, and some say that a beautiful wound-sewing maiden also sits upon the stone, which marks the very centre of the universe. Like the island itself, alatuir is a positive healing force, said to be able to give happiness to those who come into its presence. It is hardly surprising therefore, given the stone's importance, to find it has a guardian. Gagana is a large bird with an iron beak and copper claws; along with Garafena, a magical snake said to be the oldest of all snakes in existence, the two guard alatuir and keep it from harm.

There are several theories regarding the origin and location of the mythical and paradise-like Buyan. Some hold that it is a location only in myth, while other sources state that tales of Buyan actually refer to the Baltic island of Rügen. There is also a theory that the term 'buyan' was originally used as an adjective or epithet for the concept of a fabled island, only later coming to be the name of a particular island itself.

Wherever its location, Buyan has an enduring and influential place in folklore. As well as featuring in several Russian tales, in the early 20th-century Russian opera *The Tale of Tsar Saltan,* the Tsar's wife and son are mercifully saved from a watery death: cast adrift in a barrel by her jealous sisters, the pair are set ashore on Buyan by the sea, who has witnessed their plight.

Maui, Demi-god and Creator of Islands

In the rich heritage of the folklore of the Pacific, there is perhaps no better-known figure than Maui. The trickster demi-god features in many stories across the islands. Generally accepted to have been the cleverest and most mischievous of several brothers, Maui, and the lands in which his tales originated, have close links with the sea. The tales of Maui and his exploits span thousands of miles of ocean, connecting the people and cultures of New Zealand, Hawaii and the Tahitian Islands, in an invisible yet tangible web of storytelling heritage.

It was said that Maui's brothers refused to take him fishing when they set out in their canoes. Perhaps it was because he was prone to playing tricks on his slower-witted siblings. Perhaps it was because they still had not forgiven him for returning to the family as the prodigal son and gaining a place as their mother's favourite. It might simply have been the fact that Maui was just not as good as they were at catching fish and would hinder their collective efforts. Whatever the reason, one day the brothers relented and allowed him to accompany them on a fishing trip out into the rich blue waters. Maui brought with him his beloved fish-hook, baiting it with a bird that was sacred to his mother. The brothers would have no cause for complaint about this particular catch: the fish Maui managed to hook was of such a great size that he asked his brothers to help him to haul it in. Unbeknown to them, clever Maui was also pulling the very land up from the bottom of the ocean. To prevent detection, he told his brothers not to look back; unable to resist, however, one did so, this act having far-reaching consequences. Not only did the line break in that moment, but so did the land – no longer a single perfect mass, behind the canoe lay a chain of rough, uneven islands, those we know today as Hawaii.

Interestingly, thousands of miles across the ocean, this tale of Maui has a Mãori counterpart. In this version, after hiding away in the brothers' canoe, the disliked younger brother revealed himself only when it was too late to be set ashore. Although the brothers assumed he would not be able to fish without a hook, Maui produced his own and, striking his own nose and using the blood as bait, Maui was soon rewarded with the biggest bite of his life. As previously related, the land was pulled up, along with the largest fish they had ever seen. In this tale, Maui left his brothers for a time, with strict instructions not to cut into the fish, but they did not listen. The consequences were disastrous. The fish thrashed about so violently in an attempt to escape that the canoe was destroyed, the brothers killed and the land left jagged and torn, making travel across New Zealand's North Island tricky to this day.

CLAIMED BY THE WAVES: Underwater Worlds

The Lost City of Ys

Another universal idea throughout global folklore is that of the sunken or drowned city or land, lost forever beneath the waves. Common features of such tales and legends include the belief that glimpses of these tantalizing worlds can still be seen or heard today, with talk of phantom bells or ghostly music drifting over the water calling to us down through the ages.

Certainly winning the prize for the best-known land to be taken by the sea is the mythical Atlantis: first mentioned by Plato in 360BCE, the idea of the lost civilisation has continued to captivate and inspire through the ages, bringing forth further stories across time and location.

It is hardly surprising that these tales occur with such frequency, with the ravages of coastal erosion and natural disasters such as tidal waves altering and reshaping the coastlines of the world over the centuries. For some, catching sight of a now-lost land is a good thing, while others are considered a curse. Those who are unlucky enough to see Cill Stuifín in Ireland on its reappearance every seven years are said to be fated to die within the following 12 months.

The Breton legend of the lost land of Ys, or Kêr-Is, is believed to have originated in the 12th century, developing over the following centuries to detail the fall of the ill-fated city built by

King Gradlon to please his daughter, Dahut. Dahut was said to be greatly enamoured of the sea, but this proved to be something of a hindrance: Ys was built on low-lying land, and a dyke was erected to protect the city from flooding. At low tide the gate was kept open, but as the waters rose with each tide, the gate had to be closed and locked to keep the city safe. As a further precaution only one key to the gate existed, held by the king himself.

Despite her father's attempts to please her, Dahut was not said to be of good character; the young woman lived a wicked and decadent lifestyle, encouraging others to follow in her debauched ways. Dahut, according to rumour, drank, danced and fornicated, often murdering her lovers before they left her bed, and tales were rife regarding her terrible ways.

Although cautioned by Saint Winwaloe on the errors of the life she was living, Dahut remained resolutely unrepentant. As in most such tales, however, the king's daughter met her comeuppance. One day, a knight dressed all in red who was visiting Ys came to Dahut's attention. She summoned him to her chamber that night, and it might be presumed that Dahut once more had her wicked way with her handsome paramour. During the course of the night, a violent storm broke out, and Dahut told her lover about the dyke, the gate and the key. In some versions of the tale the red-clad knight (or the Devil, for so it was he) convinced Dahut to steal the key for him – in others the terrible deed is carried out by Dahut alone. The result was the same, the gate was opened wide and the high tide and storming waves rushed in, threatening to engulf Ys and all who lived there.

Alerted to the disaster, the king made good his escape upon his magical horse, taking with him his treacherous daughter. However, the very saint who had tried and failed to bring about reform in the unrepentant Dahut instructed the king to push his daughter – the demon who had brought such trouble on them all – into the water. Despite wavering, the king finally did so, before riding on to safety as the only survivor.

King Gradlon – a sadder, greyer man – found shelter in Quimper, France. A statue of him was erected there in 1858 and can still be seen today, visible between the spires of the cathedral.

The location of the ill-fated Ys is generally said to be beneath Douarnenez Bay in Brittany. Given the fluid nature of folklore however, by the 15th century the tale had relocated across the ocean, where tales began that Ys actually lay off the coast of Land's End, Cornwall. Further developments to the story in the 16th century identified this same land as Lyonnesse, the home of Tristan, of star-crossed Tristan and Isolde fame. Later tellings have further conflated the tale with King Arthur's final battle with Mordred, the land being swallowed by a tidal wave.

Fascination with sunken cities is still going strong in the 21st century with Franck Goddio's 2000 discovery of the lost Egyptian city Thonis-Heracleion. Of great strategic importance, the harbours of Thonis-Heracleion were the focus of all major trade in and out of Egypt, and the city was also of religious significance. In the 8th century CE it was lost in its entirety: the city's statues, temples and artefacts were submerged beneath the waves, preserved and remaining largely forgotten until Goddio's history-making breakthrough.

The German Atlantis: The Lost City of Vineta

Often hailed as the German Atlantis, the fate of Vineta can be read as a classic story of disaster striking as punishment for sins. Although a hospitable and polite people, according to legend the vast wealth and 'heathen-like' behaviour of the inhabitants of Vineta doomed the city to its eventual fate.

There are differing opinions on what happened to this once-marvellous city – said to be the largest in Europe for a time. One tale says that infighting and the desire for dominance of the many groups who lived within the city led to the fateful decision to ask for outside help, only for the city to be destroyed by those who had come to its aid. Another explanation is that, so displeased with what he saw, God sent the raging sea to consume the evil place in an act of Sodom and Gomorrah-style divine retribution.

As with many vanished cities, it is said that the grand silver bells of Vineta can still be heard today, ringing a warning beneath the waves. Not only that, between Good Friday and Easter Monday, when the tragedy was said to have occurred, the legend states the city itself rises from the watery depths once more, a warning to all those who may witness it of the price of wealth and vanity.

Unlike many legends, this one is dated to a specific time in history during the reign of Charlemagne, between 768 and 814. There is also considerable evidence that Vineta existed, a city with a population between 40,000 and 60,000. Mentions of this fabled lost city occur throughout history, the earliest being in the 10th century when Ibrahim ibn Yaqub referred to 'Weltaba' or 'Weltawa', meaning 'among the waves'. According to this source, Vineta had 12 gates, and was the greatest city in Europe.

Potential locations for Vineta centre around the Baltic Sea, and include off the northern German bathing resort of Koserow, east of the island of Ruden, Germany or the current location of the town of Wolin in Poland. Vineta is sometimes linked to the Viking stronghold of legend, Jomsburg or Jomsborg, which is also often said to have been located at Wolin.

The legend endures to this day: there is a board game named after the city, based loosely on the Vineta legend. Several ships of the German navy bore the name *Vineta* in the 19th and early 20th centuries. A minesweeper had the name from 1961 to 1992. The lost city has even been said to be the legendary Atlantis itself.

Archaeologist Klaus Goldmann dedicated huge time and effort in attempting to locate Vineta. Using maps and satellite photographs of the Baltic Sea and region, Goldmann and his co-author Günter Wermusch have concluded that the actual location of the historic city was in fact near Barth. The town has received an influx of visitors interested in the Vineta legend, with a Vineta museum and festival bringing many to the area. According to Goldmann, far from being inhabitants of a 'backwater of the so-called Dark Ages' as medieval northern Europe is often considered, the people of the region were highly skilled engineers; the failure of the defensive system of canals and dykes when breached by invading forces led to the watery fate of the once-proud city. Goldmann further hypothesizes that Vineta fell to a crusade led by the Catholic powers who considered its inhabitants infidels.

Urashima Tarō and the Palace of the Dragon King

Many versions of the tale of Urashima Tarō exist, yet the seeds of the story appeared in Japan as early as the 8th century. The legend goes as follows: Urashima, a young fisherman, is walking home in the twilight after a day at sea, when he sees a group of boys torturing a small turtle. Now, while Urashima is known as a most skilled fisherman, he is also famous for his kind heart, so he rescues the turtle and releases it back into the sea. He thinks nothing more of it until the next day, when he sees the turtle again. She comes into his boat to thank him for his good deed, and makes an astonishing offer: to take him to the Palace of Ryújin, the Dragon King of the Sea, where it is said that it is always a different season on each side. Urashima, of course, accepts. His day takes an even stranger turn when the turtle grows and grows until she is large enough to have him sit on her back. She carries him to the Palace of the Dragon King, deep in the depths of the ocean – yet on the way he doesn't become tired, nor do his clothes become wet.

On arrival, he is escorted through the gates of the great underwater palace by the guards, and inside sees the small turtle once more, now transformed into a lovely princess named Otohime Sama, the Daughter of the Dragon. Urashima happily decides to stay with the princess as her husband. After a time, he begins to think of his elderly mother and father and misses his childhood home. He tells his wife of his sorrow, saying that he intends to visit his parents, and then return to her in the palace of the sea. The princess tells him that she will certainly miss him, but gives her blessing, and the gift of a box as a token of their love, which contains a very precious thing that will protect him from all harm – but only on the condition that he never opens it. Urashima accepts the box, and is whisked away on the back of a turtle to be delivered safely to the shore once more.

On his arrival he sees that his home is gone, and his mother and father are nowhere to be found. Dismayed, he asks if anybody remembers the fisherman Urashima Tarō. The people there reply that they do, yet only as a character in old tales of a man who was swallowed by the sea 300 years before, and that his parents died of grief. Urashima realizes that he has not been in the Sea King's palace for just a few days, but for hundreds of years, and all he knew and loved is now gone. Overcome with grief, Urashima returns to the seashore to wait for the turtle to collect him, yet it never comes. In despair, he thinks of his bride, and turns to the box – now his only hope of uncovering the secret of where to find her. Fatefully, he opens it. In a puff of smoke the elixir of everlasting youth blows away, and the years he has lost catch up with him at once; his hair turns white, his face wrinkles and his back bends with age. There, on the same shore where he met the turtle 300 years before, he falls down dead at the edge of the sea, never again to see his love – who still waits for him in the depths of the sea, in the glorious Palace of the Dragon King.

SCHEHERAZADE'S TALES: One Thousand and One Nights

Across the world, the sea holds the promise of gifts and opportunity, yet also of threats unknown. Treasures of the sea are depicted in just this way in *One Thousand and One Nights* – or *Alf layla wa-layla* – a collection of Middle Eastern tales dating back to the Islamic Golden Age. The book uses a frame story as a backdrop to many smaller tales – famously known as the *Arabian Nights* to Western readers.

This tale tells that Shahryãr, the Sasanian king, is dismayed to find his wife has been unfaithful to him, and has her killed in revenge. He then decides to castigate all women, claiming they are all likely to be just as unfaithful. The king sets out to marry one virgin each day, consummate the marriage, and have her killed immediately on the following day, so that no wife can ever be unfaithful to him. One brave woman, Scheherazade, offers herself to the king willingly when no more virgins can be found. She comes up with a solution to prolong her life: to tell one tale to the king each night, but not give the ending until the next evening, keeping the man in suspense, and herself alive at each sunset. She can never be killed without leaving the conclusion to a tale untold, and in this way she survives for 1,001 nights. After this, versions of the tale differ, yet in all of them the woman survives at the decree of the king.

One tale from the collection, *The Fisherman and the Jinni*, reveals just how mercurial the waves can be with their gifts and dangers.

The Fisherman and the Jinni

Once there was a poor fisherman with a large family: a wife and three children. He worked hard each day, casting his nets four times, yet they often came back empty. One day was different. As he began to pull up his catch, he found it weighted down. With excitement the fisherman tried and tried to pull it up, and eventually managed to drag the net to shore. Yet, in his dismay, he found only the carcass of a donkey inside. He lost all hope, bereft that the efforts he had put into his work had amounted to nothing, and proclaimed there was nothing good left in the world but Allah himself.

He cried out praises to God, and plunged once more into the depths with his net. This time too it became heavy. And, once more, the man hoped it would be filled with fish. Yet, once more, his hopes were dashed. For there in his net lay a huge clay pitcher, filled with nothing but dirt. He prayed to God once more, asking his forgiveness, and tried a third time, throwing his nets into the sea. This time it came back filled with little other than broken pottery and glass.

Then, at last, he beseeched God to fill his nets on his fourth and final throw. Yet the net caught at the bottom of the sea, so the fisherman jumped in after it. This time he found a jar of yellow copper, stoppered with lead, and bearing the seal of King Solomon himself.

The fisherman, realizing its value, planned to sell the jar after cleaning it out. But, when he had prised out the stopper, he found nothing inside but smoke. The smoke poured out of the jar, spiralling up to the heavens until it formed a huge jinni. Recognizing it as an evil spirit, the fisherman was terrified.

The jinni believed he stood before Solomon himself, and begged the fisherman not to kill him. Yet when the man revealed his true identity, a lowly fisherman, the jinni vowed to kill him within an hour. He offered to grant him only one wish: the ability to choose the manner of his death.

The fisherman was taken aback, demanding to know why he must die. The jinni was happy to provide an explanation. He had been trapped in the jar by King Solomon. For a whole century, the jinni told himself that he would enrich his rescuer forever. Yet, then a second century passed, and during this time he vowed to offer endless wealth to anyone who released him from his prison. Over the third century, the jinni pledged three wishes to whoever freed him. By the fourth century, the jinni had grown tired and angry, and pledged that whoever brought him forth from his captivity would be put to death instantly, yet given a choice of how they would be killed.

The man begged for his life, but the jinni would not relent. A plan began to form in the fisherman's mind.

'How did you manage to fit into such a small bottle, anyway?' asked the man with the cunning of a creature facing its end.

The jinni could not resist displaying his magic. He shrank back down into nothing and, in a billow of smoke, disappeared back into the bottle, whereupon the fisherman replaced the stopper.

'Ha!' shouted the fisherman, 'Now I have you! How would you like to be thrown back into the sea for your troubles?'

And this time, it was the jinni who began to plead for forgiveness, offering to reward the man if he would only release him from his prison. In his cunning, the fisherman conceded.

The jinni rose up in a pillar of smoke as before, and this time kicked the jar into the sea. The fisherman was so afraid – and sure of his own imminent death – that it's said to this day that he wet himself in fright!

Yet the jinni was true to his bargain. He led the man through the wilderness, to a mountain pool filled to the brim with the most colourful fish he had ever laid eyes on. The fisherman eagerly cast his net into the waters. On drawing them up he found he had caught four fish, each shining brightly in a different colour.

The jinni decreed that the man should offer each of the fish up to the sultan himself. Yet, before he left to see the world, the jinni warned the man that he should never fish in the pool more than once a day. The man did as the jinni had told him, and set off at once.

The sultan was amazed. He had never seen such wondrous fish, and paid the poor fisherman a good sum of money in return for his troubles.

The fisherman, content to leave the tale here, returned to his wife and children with happiness and riches. Yet the sultan, whose fate is not yet told, ordered that the fish should be cooked immediately.

A slave girl took them, cleaned them, and placed them in a pan to fry. Yet, on turning them to cook the other side, a woman appeared in the midst of the kitchen heat wearing clothes of silk; her fingers were adorned with jewels and on her arms hung great bangles.

With a stick, she prodded at the fish in the pan, crying out, 'Oh fish, oh fish! Are you still true to your covenant?' And this she shouted three times, as the slave girl fainted away to the floor.

Finally, the fish replied, 'Yes! Yes, we are!'

And when the slave girl came back to her senses she saw that the fish were charred black in the pan, and fainted again in horror.

Soon the sultan's man came to investigate why the meal was taking so long to cook. He kicked at the girl until she came to, demanding to know what had happened, and the girl told him.

The sultan's man went to the fisherman, and demanded that he return to the mountain pool to catch four more fish to replace the last. And the fisherman did as he was commanded.

The sultan's man took the fish back to the palace, and ordered that the slave girl cook these four fish as before. This time he would see the marvel for himself. All happened exactly as before: the fish were flipped, the woman appeared, and the fish cried out to her in reply. Amazed, he ran to the sultan, recounting all that he had seen, and the sultan demanded to see the miraculous fish for himself.

The sultan's man went to the fisherman once more, this time with three witnesses, ordering him to catch four more fish. And so the man did.

This time, the king watched as they were frying, when a slave appeared in the kitchen with a branch in his hand, asking of the fish: 'Oh fish, oh fish! Are you still true to your covenant?' And this he shouted three times.

Again, the fish replied, 'Yes! Yes, we are!'

The slave strode over to the fish, toppled the pan to the ground with the branch, and promptly disappeared.

The sultan summoned the fisherman to him, demanding to know where he had caught the fish. A short time later the fisherman soon walked the path to the pool in the mountains once more, this time followed by the sultan and his men. When the sultan saw the wondrous pool, filled with fish of all colours, he was truly amazed. He vowed to uncover the secret of the pool.

The sultan changed his clothes and jewels, and began to march over the mountain. Once he had reached the other side, he began to climb the next mountain, and the next still, despite the heat and his trepidation. Soon, the sultan spotted a black dot in the distance. Convinced this was where the answer to the mystery lay, he set out to reach it.

After a time had passed he reached his destination. There he found a stone palace plated with iron. One door stood open, and the sultan proceeded to knock on it three times, but to no avail. No one answered from within, so the sultan took it upon himself to enter without invitation.

The sultan wandered through each beautiful room, admiring the gold-embellished ornaments and silk-lined walls. He marvelled at four red-gold lion fountains that stood in one courtyard as the palace birds circled freely above. While the sultan was overwhelmed by the beauty and riches of the palace, at the same time he was deeply saddened that there was no one who could tell him the secrets of the mountain pool. Yet, as he sat in his sadness, a voice began chanting from behind him, and the sultan could tell that whoever it belonged to was laden down with grief. He turned and began to trace his way through the palace, intent on finding whoever the voice belonged to.

Soon the sultan came to two heavy doors. Pushing them open, he saw a young man sitting before him, pale in the face with rosy cheeks bearing a small mole, his head adorned with a gem-filled crown. Overjoyed, the sultan ran to him.

Yet the young man did not rise, still overcome with misery.

The sultan beseeched the man to tell him the secrets of the mountain pool and his fishes. And at this the young man, in his sorrow, began to cry.

'But why do you cry?' asked the sultan, dismayed.

To this, the young man raised his silken garments. And instead of living legs, he revealed that his lower body was made entirely of stone.

The sultan's heart melted with compassion for the man. He begged him to tell not only the tale of the fishes, but his own sad story along with it. And so the young man did, by recounting 'The Tale of the Ensorcelled Prince', a tale within a tale, within a tale – as the *One Thousand and One Nights* often does.

The Tale of the Ensorcelled Prince

Once there was a prince who married his lovely cousin. Yet their marriage was far from a happy one. Unknown to the prince, the wife was skilled in sorcery and magic. Each night, the wife would give the prince a potion, and this would make him sleep through the night, while she crept away to her freedom.

One day, he overheard two slaves discussing his wife's night-time sojourns. The next evening, the prince pretended to take the potion, but did not drink it down. Then he followed his wife on her escapades.

And what he found was that his wife was, in fact, being unfaithful to him: with a slave. He immediately flew into a rage, set on killing the man. In his anger, he beat the unfaithful slave severely. Luck was on the slave's side: he lay there, almost at his end, but death still eluded him. Soon, the prince's wife came to the slave, taking him and tending to him. And this she did for the next three years. When he found out the prince was beside himself with rage. He went to his wife, demanding answers, and with every intention of killing her afterwards.

Fate turned its back on the prince. The wife mustered all she could against him, using her powers of sorcery to bind him with a magic spell. At once, the prince began to turn to stone, from his feet upwards. But once he was petrified to his waist, the spell was done. The prince was destined to be half-man, half-stone forever. And not only this, for the wife had yet more magic. She enchanted their entire city, transforming the four islands it was made of into mountains that surrounded a huge mountain pool. And she transformed people of the four faiths into fish: Muslims into white fish, Christians into blue, Jews into yellow, and Zoroastrians into red fish. To make matters worse, the wife would return to her prince each day, and whip him as he stood as still as stone. And now the tale of the sultan's speaking fish makes a lot more sense indeed!

After the tale was told, the sultan pledged to gain freedom for the prince from his plight. He helped the prince take his revenge by killing the slave, throwing his body into a well, then posing as the slave to persuade the wife to free the prince, which indeed she did. The wife then lifted all of her enchantments, restoring the city and the people to their rightful forms. Finally, still believing the sultan's disguise, the woman went to embrace him. At this, he stabbed her through, and then cleft her in half with one blow.

As for the fisherman, he was rewarded well: with a new position for his son at the sultan's palace, and the stone prince taking one of the fishermen's daughters as his wife, with the other marrying the sultan himself. And now we might do well to reflect on what such a tale might teach us: a story of a woman decreed a witch, punished for her love of another man, and then murdered by the hand of her husband.

REVERSAL OF FORTUNE: The Lady of Stavoren

The tale of het Vrouwtje van Stavoren – the Lady of Stavoren – explains the origins of a sandbar in the harbour outside Stavoren, Friesland, in the Netherlands. The appearance and growth of this natural barrier was the cause of the decline in fortunes of the city in the Middle Ages, as shipping could no longer reach the port with ease. The legend, initially quite basic, has seen many developments and variations since first appearing in the *Friesland Chronicle* by Ocko Scarlensis in 1597, and there are at least 27 versions of this tale in existence.

According to the story as it is now known, Stavoren, once a poor land, had grown to be a city of great wealth and prosperity with the advent of trade and commerce. The fortunes of Stavoren were irreparably reversed once more, however, due to the greed and bad temper of a wealthy widow who lived there. The woman, a merchant in her own right, sent one of her captains to bring her back the greatest treasure that existed in the world. He did just that, returning with grain – the main ingredient required for bread, the greatest sustaining food of every person. Far from being pleased, the lady was so angered that she had the entire lot cast overboard into the harbour, a terrible waste when there were those who were hungry in the city, begging her for some of the wheat she did not want. Taken to task for her actions, and being reminded that her fortunes could be reversed at any time, instead of being humbled the woman grew even angrier, tossing one of her rings into the water in a display of wanton defiance – she would never grow poor, unless the ring came back to her.

Of course, the ring did return to her, appearing inside a fish served at a banquet she held. Her own, and the city's, fortunes plummeted, the harbour blocked by a sandbar on which the discarded wheat – now useless – continued to grow.

In another variation, the city was submerged by a terrible flood – such an event did occur in 1657 – in punishment for the wickedness and pride of all inhabitants, and the merchant woman in particular, for discarding the grain and denying it to the poor and hungry. The harbour was, by and by, covered with long waving grass that resembled corn stalks, a graphic reminder and warning to all.

As trade dried up, so did the fortunes of Stavoren, the unfortunate city declining once more to its previously impoverished state. More mishaps followed, floods over time washing away a large portion of the town, dykes hastily built in an attempt to protect what was left.

Today, Stavoren is in size a shadow of its former self, now a village with a population of around a thousand. A statue of the ill-famed lady can be seen in Stavoren harbour, contemplating, one might say, at her leisure, the harm caused by her foolish actions. Discerning readers might question the all-too-familiar motif of a woman being held responsible for the downfall of many, reflecting on how easily such a narrative tool is, even today, accepted without question.

Top Tales from the Seven Seas

The term 'the Seven Seas' is almost as old as time itself, making an appearance as early as 4,300 years ago in a hymn to Inanna – the Sumerian goddess of love, fertility and war – written by one of her high priestesses, Enheduanna, who is the world's first author known by their actual name. While 'the Seven Seas' has meant very different things to people across the globe in different ages, people now use the phrase to mean all the oceans in the world. Let's explore some of the gods and goddesses that hail from each of the Seven Seas we know today.

I The Arctic Ocean: Sedna, the Inuit Mother of the Sea

In one version of this Indigenous traditional story, Sedna was said to be a giant with such a great hunger that she attacked her parents one night and began eating their limbs. Outraged, her father took her out in his kayak, and threw her over the side. Yet Sedna refused to die; and as she held on fiercely to the side, her father promptly cut off her fingers and thumbs. Sedna sank down into the depths to rule the Underworld forever, and her severed digits became all the marine animals of the seas.

2 The North Atlantic Ocean: The Old Woman Arnaquagsaq

In Greenland, the sea goddess is named Arnaquagsaq – the very great or old woman. She sits in her dark dwelling in the depths of the ocean, while a bowl catches the oil that drips down the sides of her only lamp. The Inuit people of Greenland see this lamp as the sun, while the bowl is the great ocean that stretches out beneath it, holding all of the food-animals of the seas. It's said that when times are harsh, and there is little food, Arnaquagsaq is plagued by parasites, and only the spiritual journeying and prayers of the angakok priests can help her. Yet the priests face great challenges in reaching her. First, a priest must pass through Arsissut, the realm of the happy dead, then cross a great abyss containing a constantly turning wheel as slippery as ice. Next, he must pass a boiling kettle with seals in it, until finally arriving at a house protected by fearsome creatures – either seals or dogs. Once inside, the priest must face the final obstacle: a bridge as thin as a knife's edge. The prayers that are offered up are seen as great weather magic, which chase away the storm clouds that often appear later in the season. Only then will Arnaquagsaq release all of the food-animals back to the people, and there is a time of plenty again.

3 The South Atlantic Ocean: Iemanjá, the Candomblé Goddess of the Sea

Known by many names, Iemanjá, Yemanjá or Janaína is an orixá, or goddess, worshipped in the Candomblé and Umbanda religions across Brazil. She is seen as Queen of the Ocean, often depicted as a woman rising from the waves, and associated with the bountiful fertility of the seas. The orixá has power over all things to do with being a woman, including motherhood and children. She is the patron of fishermen, aiding them in their catch, along with those who have survived shipwrecks. Light blue or white are her colours, and her followers often deck themselves in white dresses, throwing white roses into the waters in her honour. Mirrors and combs are her symbols.

Iemanjá is a figure who came to Brazil with the enslaved Africans brought to its shores. In the African Yoruba tradition she is the orisha Yemoja, a mother spirit who rules over waters, rivers and streams, often depicted as a mermaid. Some statues today show Iemanjá herself as a mermaid, yet many, strangely, also depict her as a slender white woman. This is explained easily: when her followers arrived in Brazil they used religious syncretism to help them to continue the worship of their own orishas in the face of suppression; this is when one deity or spirit is amalgamated with another, local version to aid their acceptance. They began to celebrate Iemanjá on the existing Brazilian saints' days, and today her festival is still held across Brazil on 2 February – the date of the official holiday of Nossa Senhora dos Navegantes (Our Lady of the Naviagtors). The largest of these festivals is held in Salvador, the capital of the state of Bahia, where her statue is carried amidst thronging crowds. Flowers, candles and toy boats are released as offerings into the sea in her honour, carrying wishes and prayers of the supplicants along with them as they move across the waves. Similar festivities happen on 8 December at the Festa da Conceição da Praia (Feast of Our Lady of Conception). During the de-Africanization of Afro-Brazilian culture, the orixás – spirits or forces of nature that do not take human form – became personified in human-like statues. Iemanjá took on a form very similar to the Virgin Mary: slender, dressed in light blue with pale skin. There has been a movement to make the figure more African by giving her black skin, and a fuller figure to show her links to fertility and womanhood. Many dispute this movement, claiming there is no racism in the syncretized iconography. The debate continues today, as the expression of this religious figure morphs and changes with each person and generation that follow her.

4 The Indian Ocean: The Great Dragon of the Primordial Seas

Naga Padoha is a great dragon that rules the Underworld and primordial sea in Indonesia, and the opponent of the great creator-god, Mula Jadi Na Bolon, who existed before humans were created when the world began. The birth of humanity actually arose when Mula Jadi's granddaughter fled from her lizard-shaped husband in horror, rousing the sympathy of her grandfather, who offered the girl a handful of earth on which to live. This earth was mistakenly spread out near the fearsome sea dragon, who almost destroyed it with his writhing and churning, and the girl could find no peace. Yet armed with her own shrewdness, and the help of her grandfather, the girl overcame the dragon, running him through with a sword and casting him in an iron block. Now, whenever the bound dragon writhes in his prison, an earthquake wreaks havoc on the land.

5 The North Pacific Ocean: Hit, the Octopus Goddess of Micronesia

On the Caroline Islands, Hit is a beautiful goddess that takes octopus form. The most famous tale recounts how Hit's daughter became the mistress of one of the gods. Yet each time the god tried to meet with his mistress, his sky-wife would not be far behind. Hit took it upon herself to dance as a distraction, giving such a wild and erotic performance that the wife was overcome. She fainted with sheer excitement, and was carried back to her home in the sky. So successful was this plan that Hit committed to the show each time her daughter intended to meet her lover, leading to the conception of Olifat, one of the Caroline Island's most beloved folk heroes.

For the Itneg of the Philippines, the sea itself is sentient. At the beginning of time, only the sea and the sky existed. Traditional stories recount how a kite, having no place to settle, caused the sea to wage war against the sky. She threw her waters up towards the sky, which caused the heavens to make a pact of peace with her. Afterwards, the sky decided to enact his revenge: with a great display of power, the sky rained down huge clods of earth on to the waters, which became islands. The sea was subdued, and was never able to rise up against the sky again, and was destined to run only back and forth forever. This is how the world was created. Some people tell a similar tale to explain the movement of the sea; in it the ancient sea god Magindang endlessly lusts after the youthful god of the pale moon, and so each month the waves rise up to catch him.

6 The South Pacific Ocean: Te Mãngõroa, the Shark of the Milky Way

For the last 50 years, the Mãori of Aotearoa New Zealand have been fighting to reclaim their heritage after facing years of racism and intolerance; this includes their traditional astronomical knowledge of the stars, both for navigating the seas – *tãtai arorangi* – yet also of celestial knowledge relating to Creation, the gods and about the seasons and time itself: *Kauwae-runga*. As often happens in oral traditions, this knowledge has been kept and passed down from generation to generation using traditional sayings, songs and stories. These Indigenous tales of the heavens have an unexpected link to the waters of the earth.

The sea is seen as vital in Mãori culture, as the source of food, and of life itself. In the Indigenous creation epic, Ranginui is the Sky and Papatúãnuku, his consort, is the Earth. They have many children, and among them is Tangaroa, the god of the sea: the sea has been central to Mãori life from the very beginning of time.

Sharks are considered sacred guardians to many, and appear in a large number of traditional tales. One *taniwha* – guardian creature or monster – is Ruamano, who is said to take the form of a mako shark. Tales tell how he rescues sailors from overturned canoes – *waka* – taking them to dry land, and safety.

It is said that the traditional hero and demi-god Maui placed the shark, Te Mãngõroa, up in the sky, and this became the Milky Way. Today, it is still referred to as Te Ikaroa (the long fish), Te Ikanui (the great fish) and Te Mãngõroa (the long mango shark) because of its fish-like shape.

7 The Southern (or Antarctic) Ocean

Since few people live in the Southern Ocean other than at research station outposts, it follows that tales of gods and goddesses are rare. However, you might be surprised to learn that the Southern Ocean was once thought to contain its own mysteries, and its folklore is extensive. It was once believed that a vast continent, *Terra Australis Incognita*, must exist somewhere in this icy sea in order to balance the landmasses in the north, and many explorers set out to find it in the 16th and 17th centuries. As we know today, this longing for a lost continent has still not been satiated, and the ice sheets of Antarctica belong only to the whales and the penguins. And of course the Ningen – creatures that many websites say have been sighted in the Southern Ocean; rumour tells that sightings are reputedly being taken very seriously by the Japanese government. Some staff members on whale research ships have reported that the creatures resemble blubbery, white, whale-like masses, and are humanoid creatures with grasping hands, and tails instead of legs. Could these creatures really lurk in the vast, uninhabited expanse that is the Southern Ocean? Maybe we'll never know.

RED SKY AT NIGHT: Sailor Superstitions from Across the Globe

With the perilous nature of sea voyages and the uncertainties that prevailed when setting off for waters unknown, it comes as no surprise that numerous superstitions and beliefs have grown up among those who lived their lives on the waves. For despite the treacherous nature of the sea, there were many ways a canny sailor could guard against misfortune, and even more actions and mistakes that needed to be avoided at all cost.

Some people were thought to be naturally luckier than others, and protected at sea. Those who were 'born with a caul' – that is, with a portion of tissue or amniotic membrane attached to their head – were said to be safe from death by drowning. Some believed that this immunity only held for that person, while others stated the protection could be transferred – hence a thriving trade in preserved cauls right up until the 20th century. One particular tale tells of how a child born with this protection caused no end of trouble to his mother at bath time – however hard she tried, the air-filled buoyancy of his caul meant that she couldn't keep him long enough under the water to be properly washed. To be born in the caul was to be in good company; among the great and famous reputed to have been born thus are Byron, Freud, James I and Napoleon. Cicero is often cited as stating that those born at the rising of the Dog Star, Sirius – that is, 3 July to 11 August – were never to be drowned, protected by the accident of their birth.

There has been much concern regarding the luck or otherwise of particular days when it comes to setting sail. In England and

Scotland, Sundays were seen as a lucky day to do so, and a voyage beginning on that day would go without a hitch. Wednesday and Thursday were likewise lucky according to Norse tradition, being associated with Odin and Thor respectively and thus, it was thought, invoking the protection of the god in question. Friday, on the other hand, has been considered an unlucky day for sea journeys in many cultures. The obvious and most frequent connection made is that of it being the day of Christ's crucifixion, and it has also been suggested by some that, being the day of the Norse goddess Freya, with her association with the much-maligned cat (see below), it was therefore unlucky for those at sea. On the other hand, Friday was said to be an auspicious day to start a voyage in America, due to many positive events in the history of that nation occurring on that day. For Spanish sailors, Tuesday was a bad day to set sail, as outlined in the proverb *'El Martes, ne te casas, ne te embarques, ne de te mujer apartarse'* – 'Tuesday, don't marry, go to sea, or leave your wife'.

Perhaps not surprisingly, the number of things that were seen as unlucky at sea were more numerous than those that brought favour. It was well known that having a woman on board a ship was seen as a sure-fire way to bring bad fortune (both for the ship and no doubt the woman in question) although, conversely, it has been said that a naked woman actually has the opposite effect and could calm a storm from on deck.

Making a wine-glass ring would cause the death of a sailor, and if the glass actually broke, then any number of disasters could occur. Whistling close to the sea could have perilous consequences, as could anything going wrong during the naming of a ship. Although red sky the night before setting sail could be seen as a positive sign, if it happened come morning, that was another matter entirely and the sailor should beware of what might be about to befall him.

Cats were said to be used by witches to cause storms that put the crews of ships in peril, while in Zoroastrian folklore cats are thought to have been created when a woman copulated with a demon, and it is believed that all the fish will die if a cat dares to urinate in the water.

Haunting the Waves: Ghostly Ships and Skeleton Crews

The sea is calm. The moon shines on the gently bobbing waves. Suddenly, out of nowhere, sails can be seen, ropes heard thrumming in the rising wind. The ghost ship sails into view, onlookers watching in amazement or terror as it rushes towards them, only to vanish once more before their very eyes.

Legends of phantom ships that haunt the seas of the world are widespread across the globe, providing universal appeal and fascination. Some of these ships are purely fictional in origin, with no known historical ship to correspond to the tale that has built up around it. Legends of *The Flying Dutchman*, believed to have originated in the 17th century, are perhaps the most famous of these: the ill-fated vessel doomed to sail the seas for eternity, never able to come into port. Others can be verified as having been a historical vessel, overcome by an unexplained and terrible fate. These ships continue to be sighted long after the untimely demise of their crews, often on the anniversary of the tragedy.

The *Mary Celeste* is one such ship. She was discovered on 5 December 1872 off the Azores in the Atlantic Ocean, in perfect condition but without any sign of her crew or what had become of them; by definition truly a ghost ship – a vessel discovered without its crew. Despite a vast amount of interest and investigation, no satisfactory explanation has ever been found. The *Mary Celeste* has been sighted many times during the following decades, entering folklore and popular culture as 'the greatest maritime mystery of all time'.

New ghost ships continued to enter the existing catalogue of phantom vessels well into the 20th century. According to legend, the SS *Ourang Medan*, a ship of Indonesian origin, met an unknown fate in the Dutch East Indies. In 1947 the ship gave out a distress call, but when help arrived, it was to find everyone on board dead. Not only that, their faces were frozen in expressions of eternal horror. Although there are various explanations, from the mundane to the paranormal, the ultimate fate of the crew is unknown, and even the existence of the ship itself is yet to be satisfactorily proven.

Perhaps one of the most intriguing tales of a ghostly vessel is that of the *Caleuche* – believed to mean to change condition, or to be another – a phantom ship that is a staple of the rich folklore of Chiloé. The series of islands lies off the coast of Chile, and it was here, during the arrival of the Spanish in the mid-16th century, that the first sightings of this mysterious ship were reported.

The *Caleuche* is said to be quite a sight indeed: brightly lit and with music that drifts across the waves, the atmosphere is one of partying, fun and cheer. The crew, however, are no ordinary sailors; the ship is manned by witches and wizards, and also, it is said, by those who have lost their lives to the treacheries of the sea. Those on board are free from the constraints of human illness and the ravages of age do not touch them; as the name of the vessel suggests, the ability to shapeshift is also attributed to those onboard. This has created an almost veneration for sea creatures and birds in the Chilote people, as they could be the souls of the departed. Sightings of the *Caleuche* tend to take place at night near beaches, and there are tales of the ship transporting sailors to other islands, and also of the ship pretending to be another ship before discarding the disguise and vanishing – much to the amazement of onlookers.

There is another, darker, side to the *Caleuche*. To see the ship is to risk one's very existence; those who have witnessed the spectacle might be taken on board to join the eternal party, or find themselves left behind, but without speech or their sanity. There is also a fear that a *Caleuche* sailor can kidnap or kill an onlooker; and, just for catching sight of the ship, an unwary fisherman could be physically altered and taken on board to serve.

As with most ghost ships, various theories have been put forward to try to explain the many sightings of the *Caleuche* that have spanned history and continue to occur to this day. Mirages, glowing marine plant life and UFOs are among those mooted, but there is one of particular note because it is held by the Chilote themselves. It is said that the *Caleuche* stories are an afterlife narrative for those who have lost loved ones to the sea, providing comfort amid their grief that existence continues in some form aboard the eternally partying ship; this is, perhaps, the most satisfying explanation of all.

THE GRAVEYARD OF THE ATLANTIC: The Mystery of the Bermuda Triangle

The folklore of the seas is full of terrifying creatures and seductive spirits ready to lure the unwary to their doom. Perhaps even more terrifying is the unseen threat that strikes without warning, leaving no trace of those who fall foul of an invisible force.

The Bermuda Triangle, an area in the Atlantic Ocean loosely framed by Miami, Puerto Rico and Bermuda, is well famed for being a place of tragedy. According to legend, ships and planes crossing this area have completely disappeared into thin air, the men, women and children onboard swallowed up by whatever invisible force is at work there.

An article in the *Miami Herald* on 17 September 1950 by E.V.W Jones is the first known source to suggest something strange was occurring in the area now popularly known as the Bermuda Triangle, listing several boats and planes that had seemingly vanished there. It was 14 years later, however, in 1964, that Vincent Gaddis elaborated on this evidence and put forward a concrete theory that strange happenings were occurring in 'The Deadly Bermuda Triangle'. Referring to the 'mysterious menace' that had destroyed 'hundreds' of planes and ships without a trace, Gaddis traced these incidents back to the middle of the 19th century, with the disappearance of the *Rosalie* in 1840 being one of the earliest. Gaddis even went so far as to allege that almost a thousand lives had been claimed by the triangle.

The most famous and often-cited disappearance in the ill-fated triangle is that of the lost patrol or, as it is popularly known, Flight 19. On 5 December 1945, five TBM Avenger torpedo bombers took off from Florida on a routine patrol. The intended flight plan should have taken around 2 hours, but 1 hour 45 minutes after take-off, a startling communication came from the patrol leader. They were off course and could not see land. Furthermore, despite the fact all were experienced pilots, they could not even identify which way west lay, and the sea below looked strange and unfamiliar. The tower listened, helpless, as conversation between the pilots grew steadily more frantic. The last words heard were, 'Tower, we are not certain where we are … we think we must be about two hundred and twenty-five miles north-east of base. It looks like we are –'. And then, nothing but silence. Not only was the doomed patrol never found, but a Martin Mariner – a weighty vehicle crewed by 13 men that went to their aid – also vanished.

Such tales, repeated and embroidered, have become the steadfast 'facts' of the Bermuda Triangle mystery. There have been numerous criticisms and debunking attempts, however, with critics pointing out several flaws in the seemingly watertight accounts. In 1975, Larry Kusche published *The Bermuda Triangle Mystery: Solved*, in which he highlighted various problems with the work of Gaddis and others. According to Kusche, exaggeration, inaccurate reporting and flat-out fabrication significantly muddied the waters, especially the omission of references to inclement weather conditions at the time of some disappearances. It has also been pointed out by sceptics that, given how busy those waters are, the number of disappearances and accidents is statistically even somewhat on the low side.

Explanations for the supposed mystery of the Bermuda Triangle range from the bizarre to the mundane. Technology left from Atlantis and UFOs (the latter popularized by Charles Berlitz) are among the more outlandish suggestions that have received attention over the years. Natural phenomenon such as compass variations, the effects of the Gulf Stream and violent weather conditions have found popularity among those looking for a more scientific theory, along with the obvious and perhaps most tragic contender, human error.

The fate of Flight 19 and the other planes and vessels that have vanished will likely never be discovered. It is this very uncertainty, along with the prevailing allure of the unknown, that ensures the continuation of the enduring fascination of the Bermuda Triangle.

OF COFFINS, ROGUES AND PRIESTS: Smuggling Around England's Coasts

Tales of black-hearted smugglers and violent deeds abound through the history and folklore of the United Kingdom, nowhere more so than in the West Country areas of England. In Devon and Cornwall, fact blends seamlessly with fiction to create some of the most enduring and compelling smuggling-related lore in those counties.

The golden days of the smuggling trade took place between 1700 and 1850, with various places along the English coast making perfect landing spots for illicit goods. Smugglers, despite frequently receiving a bad press through the ages, were actually often protected within a local community; the excise men sent to deal with them were generally despised while the lawbreakers themselves were seen as almost local heroes. Indeed, according to one source, 'the ordinary smuggler was often a fine rebellious fellow, courageous, resourceful'; in effect, a far cry from the vicious brute one would expect.

Isaac Gulliver remains one of the most well-known smugglers of the West Country. Throughout his career he had managed to avoid the dreaded excise men on numerous occasions, but, as is so often the way, his luck finally appeared to be running out. Pursued one day with the excise officials close on his heels, Gulliver made it to the safety of his house, saved only by the fact that they didn't have a warrant that permitted them to follow him inside. The men were not to be deterred, however, and settled grimly to wait for their prize; with the house watched so that Gulliver couldn't escape, they waited patiently for the paper that would allow them to enter.

When it finally arrived several days later, the triumphant excise men knocked at the door, only to be faced with a disconsolate Mrs Gulliver. Their triumph turned to shame as they were led into the house, where they were shown the cold still body of Gulliver himself laid out in a coffin. No doubt apologizing profusely, they quickly left the grieving widow and the man they had come to arrest. Things were not as they seemed, however, as Gulliver instantly made a miraculous recovery; the rogue leapt from the coffin, quickly filled it with smuggled goods, and used his final resting place as a cover for conveying his booty to its intended destination.

Gulliver died in 1822, after a long and profitable career, at the end of which he was worth £60,000 and had gained enough respectability to have his final resting place in Wimborne Minster. He was also reputed to have been a spy, though for the English rather than, as many smugglers were reported to have done, turning and working for the French enemy. One legend even maintains that Gulliver saved the king himself: if the story is to be believed, he received a royal pardon for his loyalty.

Smuggling was not entirely a male-dominated activity; women were occasionally known to participate in the shadier activities of the contraband trade. For a start, the tale of Granny Grylls, who used to be known in her younger days for walking frequently with her small baby in her arms. When an official remarked on the fact that the infant was so quiet, she replied that might be the case, but she was in fact full of spirit. Never was a truer word spoken, as the 'baby' was in fact a jar containing brandy.

It was also not unheard of for a woman to be a smuggler captain in her own right: Bessie Catchpole from Essex made a reputation for herself in the trade, being in command of her own ship after she took over from her husband when he was killed.

After an initial brief power struggle in which she proved herself more than capable of holding her ground, Bessie was accepted as captain of the *Sally* without further question by the crew.

Another unlikely sounding but common group that was linked to smuggling were the local clergy. Far from condemning the activities of the smugglers, if accounts are to be believed, many men of the cloth were often right in the thick of things, either aiding smugglers and helping them to avoid detection, or participating directly themselves. The clergy of Sussex were, it seems, particularly partial to swapping their silence for a share in illegal goods, and in Burwash the parson obligingly pretended to be ill and thus remained at home on the very same day a cargo of wanted goods was being stashed among the pews of his church in order to avoid the dreaded excise men. In another instance, the vicar of Morwenstowe is said to have shocked a visitor not local to the area by being central to a retrieval operation, holding the light himself so that those who were rescuing the illicit goods from the waves could see what they were doing.

It is to be expected, therefore, that legends grew up around this notorious trade. The smugglers used this to their advantage, and it has been suggested that they started such tales themselves in order to dissuade the overly curious from straying too close to their haunts. While many smugglers and their associates are verified by the historical record, some, such as the figure known as Cruel Coppinger, are probably just a figure of legend. Coppinger is said to have appeared off the coast of Welcombe, Devon. When his ship went down in a terrible storm, Coppinger swam to shore, causing great consternation when he leapt onto the horse of a wealthy local heiress and rode off with both horse and heiress before anyone could protest. In due course he married her, and became the head of a gang of smugglers and pirates, terrorizing men both on land and at sea in his ship the *Black Prince*. When, after several years, he was finally in danger of being caught, Coppinger escaped to sea once more – the twist in the tale being that the ship he boarded was said to have vanished before the very eyes of onlookers, and neither ship nor Coppinger were ever seen again.

Will you hear of Cruel Coppinger?
He came from a foreign land;
He was brought to us by the salt water,
He was carried away by the wind!

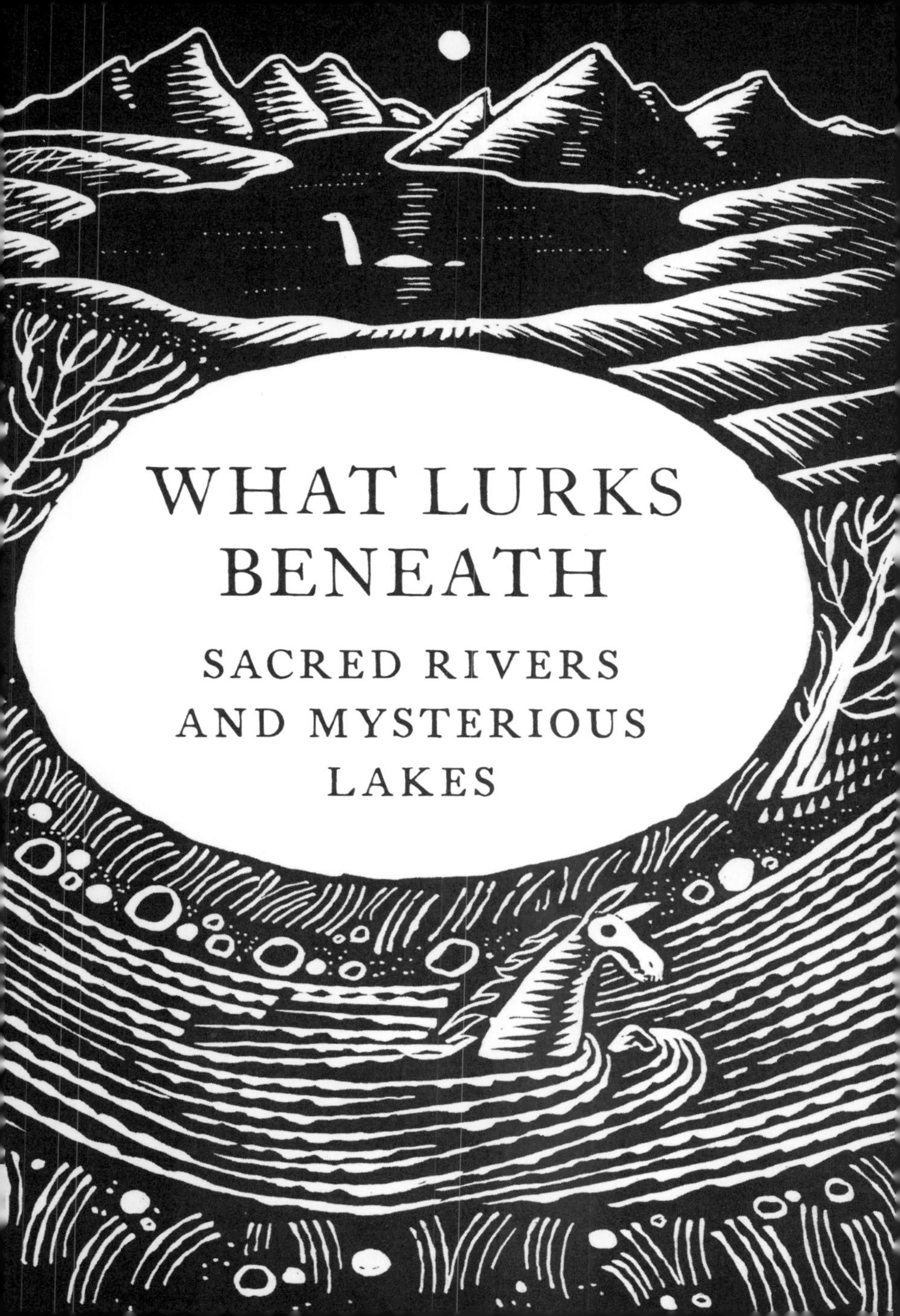
WHAT LURKS
BENEATH
SACRED RIVERS
AND MYSTERIOUS
LAKES

RIVERS AND LAKES

Rivers hold a great deal of symbolic meaning across the globe. In folklore, they often transport us, both physically and metaphorically, helping us transcend both worlds and states of being. Gods and goddesses take on their form, and use them to travel to our earthly realm, while other rivers fall from the heavens themselves. Even uttering the name of the River Ganges helps people move from life to death more peacefully, and bathing in this river is an act of purification. The rite of baptism in Christian doctrine uses lakes and pools to transform the believer from a state of sin to a state of being cleansed, making them a member of the Christian faith and presenting the opportunity to enter through the gates of heaven. In many tales, rivers symbolize the journey towards a goal and the struggle along the way: the river in *Siddhartha*, Hermann Hesse's 1922 novel, represents the path to enlightenment.

Rivers are boundaries and barriers, yet we can transgress these, with the help of the gods and their rituals. In myth and legend they help us travel between worlds or spiritual realms. The rivers of the Underworld accompany the dead on their journey through Hades in Greek myth, and in Scandinavian lore one must wade through rivers on a journey to the land of the dead. In traditional Sámi tales of Finland and Sweden, double-bottomed *sáiva* lakes act as doorways to their Underworld, with shamans able to speak to the spirits of the lakes, who could help protect people and ensure a plentiful fishing haul if offerings were left for them.

Even in literature, many authors use pools as a literary device – in *The Magician's Nephew*, C.S. Lewis filled the 'Wood between the Worlds' with pools that led to different realms, and all one had to do was jump in to be transported to a different place. In geography rivers act as physical boundaries; yet, in Irish tradition, it's said that ghosts and spirits cannot cross running water, so all one needs to do if pursued by such ghouls is to jump over a river to safety. Many people from Christian traditions know the tale of St Christopher, who performed the service of carrying people across a particularly dangerous river. One day, he helped a child by lifting him high upon his shoulders and fording the torrent. The child became so heavy that the saint struggled under the strain of carrying him. On reaching the other side, St Christopher commented on his weight. The child replied that the man had not just taken on the burden of the child himself, but the weight of the whole world, along with its creator.

Lakes and pools offer both physical and spiritual sustenance, yet secret knowledge and miraculous gifts come from the beings of lakes, wells and pools: prophecies, new skills, youth. The Lady of the Lake gives the sword Excalibur to Arthur; musical skills are bestowed by the fossegrim and other water beings. Yet often a sacrifice has to be made to receive such rewards: in Norse tales, the god Odin must sacrifice an eye to drink of the waters of the well of Mímir and gain its wisdom, while the god Heimdall gives his ear. For mere mortals, lake and river tales in folklore reveal how seeking hidden knowledge – and looking at that which is not meant for human eyes – has a price that must be paid.

When we look into a pool we see our faces staring back at us, like the mythic Narcissus. Yet the creatures of these pools also reflect our true, inner nature back at us. These water beings are changeable and fluid, with a dualistic nature. We are never sure what to expect and must treat them carefully, with reverence: they are fickle, and can bestow gifts, yet take them away just as easily as they are given. This gift-giving is often imbued with a sense of morality and expectation: these creatures choose to have faith in humankind, and believe in their innate goodness, and it is only people's own folly that leads to these gifts being taken away; but the stories always begin from a place of trust and a chance is always given. There is often a sadness when the gift needs to be taken back, or a rage at humanity's inability to be better than their nature allows. River spirits and creatures challenge humanity to be the best we can be, and are saddened by our failures; we can only wonder if we have populated our myths and legends with agents of justice, through which to judge ourselves. Often, we can see each episode with a river or lake as an opportunity to choose the correct path; to follow our higher nature, where we keep our word – unlike Melusine's husband in the French tale, who breaks his word and pays the price. Even the fearsome Japanese kappa offers a fierce respect, and challenges us as an equal sparring partner. The pink dolphin is a lesson to young women, that they will be cursed with an unwanted child if they do not behave well, refuse their animalist nature and keep their chastity, as cultural mores dictate.

Lake and river folklore also shows us that nature is cruel: all across the world, rivers are famous for taking sacrifices – particularly children. From the river hags of northern England – Jenny Greenteeth in Liverpool and Lancashire; Peg Powler of Yorkshire and Durham – to Maria Enganxa, the water hag of Majorca, who haunts wells and watering holes in the same way. All of these creatures warn small children off, and keep them safe from drowning in the dark depths. Water spirits appear throughout Germanic lore and Scandinavia as the neck, nixie and nokken, often shapeshifters by nature, many of whom lurk in ponds and lakes, dark shadowy creatures peering out from just above the waterline. Many types love music, and they are often said to lure people to their deaths, like sirens. Some require annual sacrifices, while for the nix of the Diemel in Germany an annual offering of bread and fruit is sufficient. Yet even Grimm comments on how river spirits take bloodthirstiness to a level not rivalled by spirits of any other landscape: not mountain spirits, nor those of the woodlands, and certainly not those who appear in our houses and villages. However, the nix are not seen as entirely evil, and while their cries are omens of a drowning, some believe that they lead the drowned to their own dwellings, and look after their souls, keeping them safe in upturned pots, rather than luring people to their deaths. Of course, everyone knows that iron is the enemy of the fair folk, and water spirits are no exception. When bathing in Norway, simply utter this rhyme for safety:

'Nyk! Nyk! Naal i vatn.
Jomfru Maria kastet styaal i vatn!
Du sæk, æk flyt!'

MEANING:

'Nick! Nick! Needle in water.
Virgin casteth steel in water!
Thou sink, and I flee!'

Rivers and lakes are the things of the sea, but tamed; they have similar dangers, but their dangers are tempered, and humans are offered a choice, a forked path, through which to choose our fate. If we fail, we will metaphorically be lost in our human frailty, and the gifts and wisdom of the otherworld and its gods are taken from us. They offer opportunities to transcend our lower selves, and raise us up to be godly, with super-human powers and skills. They show us the amazing things that are on offer to us, and there for the taking – if only we choose to act with wisdom and kindness, and do things in the correct way. Yet they show how we will be left bereft and godless if we choose badly.

Learn the lessons of the river beings contained in these pages; accept their wisdom and otherworldly gifts, and choose to walk in the shadow of the divine, transcending world and human boundaries. And choose well, for you will face the vengeance of the water beings if you fail …

SACRED RIVERS

Water is a source of life that we cannot live without, so it's no surprise that rivers across the globe have been considered sacred for thousands of years. While many are heavily polluted, pilgrims and the faithful still flock to their banks in countries all over the world to give thanks with votive offerings, to ask for healing, or simply to offer their prayers to the deities that the rivers call their own.

In the 15th century, the Incas saw the great Urubamba River that churns near Machu Picchu as a reflection of the Milky Way, which in itself was seen as a celestial river that draws water from its earthly counterpart. The sacred nature of rivers is no less relevant to many people today: the Whanganui was the first river in the world to be awarded the status of being a legal person by the parliament of New Zealand in 2017, in recognition of the special relationship the Māori in the region have with the river, and reflected in a local saying, 'I am the river, and the river is me.' This means that nature can now be regarded as a person, and have the same right to protection – which can be enforced. In the same year, the Uttarakhand High Court in India declared the Ganges and Yamuna rivers as 'living entities' in the same way. While this decision was reversed a few months later, with the Supreme Court decreeing that the rivers were not in fact living entities, the case highlights that the debate about the nature of rivers and their spirits is at the forefront of people's minds.

While there are seven sacred rivers in Hinduism, the Ganges is the most famous, running through both India and Bangladesh. It's said that chanting the name of the river near the dying allows their souls to pass through the gates of heaven. Bathing in the river is a holy act, which serves to cleanse people from their sins, and liberate them from *samsāra*: the cycle of life, death and rebirth. One of the largest pilgrimages in the world takes place in January when crowds – over a million people in 2017 – gather for the Makar Sankranti festival at Sagar Island, near the Bay of Bengal. This number is only surpassed by the Kumbh Mela, the largest pilgrimage in the world, which appears on UNESCO's Representative List of the Intangible Cultural Heritage of Humanity.

Many rivers are perceived as goddesses, from the Nile in Egypt to the Huang He (Yellow River) and Yangtze in China, and this is also true for the Ganges: there are lots of origin myths for the waters, yet many believe they originated when the goddess Ganga herself came down to earth in the form of a river. The goddess is said to have four arms and three eyes that enable her to see the past, present and future all at once, and she rides a white crocodile. For a river sacred to so many, and integral to life in the region, it's devastating to hear the official figures for river pollution in the Ganges: the E. coli bacteria from human sewage is over 100 times the limit deemed acceptable by the Indian government in some parts. Sadly, the endangered Ganges river dolphin purportedly represents the purity and holiness of the river, as it's said to only be able to survive in pure waters.

RIVERS OF THE UNDERWORLD

For many of us, the Underworld conjures images of echoing caves, cavernous and empty, stalactites drip-dripping into pools where shadows flicker as sea serpents glide in their timeless depths. We will one day join the lines of hopeless souls trudging the well-worn path to the creaking gates that conceal the final mysteries of life, watched over by gatekeepers that reach out to us from millennia of eerie death-tales. All too soon we will see the bejewelled thrones of Hades of Greek myth, or that of Ereshkigal, the Mesopotamian ruler of the land of the dead. We might crouch in fear at the thought of harpies soaring above us, human vultures who carry away souls from the earth to the cold chasm of death. We too might reach down to our pockets, or into our mouths, to check if we have the required coin to pay the ferryman for our final journey.

We are not far wrong with these images, for this is the picture that mythology – many mythologies – teach us: the truths of this chthonic journey into death that haunts us in the dark waking hours of the night, tossing and turning, wondering if maybe we alone can escape the grip of the Underworld like the woeful Persephone.

We see the same images arise in many death tales: that of the Greek hero Orpheus; the Norse Baldr; Hutu who won back his love, Pare, from Hine-nui-te-põ, the Mãori goddess of darkness and death. One tale less well-known is that of the twin heroes Xbalanque and Hunahpu, who travelled to Xibalba to defeat the lords of death in the Mayan Underworld – later becoming the Sun and Moon of the heavens in the *Popol Vuh,* the 16th-century cultural narrative of the K'iche' people of Guatemala.

Greek

Many myths tell us that we will soon reach a river that encircles the Underworld – or separates it from the realm of the living – on our way to the land of the dead. In Greek mythology, this is the Acheron, the river of pain. It is here that Charon, the ferryman, silently steers his murky craft through the waters for eternity. Virgil describes him as a figure 'terrible in his squalor' with 'unkempt, hoary hair', eyes that are flaming orbs and dressed only in rags that hang from his shoulders. According to Virgil, the soul of the deceased must carry an obol – Charon's obol – under their tongue as payment to the grim ferryman for bearing their souls across the river to the Underworld on his dark ferryboat. Strangely, the *Suda*, a 10th-century Byzantine encyclopaedia, gives a different image of the river: 'Acheron is like a place of healing, not a place of punishment, cleansing and purging the sins of humans.' Once more, we see rivers as a place of purification, even in death.

The Styx is often confused and conflated with the Acheron, and some say that Charon is tied to this river instead. The Styx circles the Underworld seven times and is very different to the Acheron. The *Suda* says it is a dead river, as it is all dried up, while Homer calls it the 'Water of Terror'. Some say it is a river in Arcadia, the northern Peloponnese, a 'down-flowing' river that can cause death to anyone who drinks it, yet with wonderful properties: the water will break anything made from glass, crystal or pottery, and corrode anything made from metal; gold is immune. The only thing strong enough to carry this water is the hoof of a horse. Homer says it is a river in Hades, as well as the name of the goddess Styx, daughter of Oceanus.

Many other rivers snake through the Greek Underworld: the Lethe is the river of oblivion, while the Phlegethon is the river of burning, along which 'those deserving of punishments go away and dwell'. Those deserving of punishment also 'go away' along the Cocytus, the river of lamentations and dirges, which is the opposite of the Phlegethon, and said to be very cold.

Korean

There is also a river that separates the Underworld in a well-known Korean myth from Jeju Island: Chasa Bonpuli. Here, the hero Gangnim Doryeong is tasked with capturing Yeomra, King of the Underworld. He must cross the Henggimot Lake, which is surrounded by spirits who – starved for eras and unable to enter the Underworld – attack him. Gangnim throws himself into the lake to escape, and on emerging he finds he has indeed reached the Yeonchu Gate: the entrance to the Underworld, where he defeats Yeomra's 30,000 soldiers and captures the King of the Underworld with a steel chain.

Norse

There are mutterings of an Underworld river in Norse mythology too. Snorri Sturluson briefly tells us of Gjöll in his *Gylfaginning*, the river closest to the gates of Hel over which the Gjallarbrù bridge stands. In the story of Hermódr rescuing Baldr from Hel, it's said that this bridge is thatched with glittering gold, guarded by the maiden Módgudr, and must be crossed on the way to Hel. The Norwegian ballad *Draumkvæde* tells of the journey of Olav Åsteson into the otherworld. On falling asleep on Christmas Eve, he dreamed of the fate of the dead and their final journey, taking them across the bridge Gjallarbrù – which might seem familiar to those who know the work of Charles Dickens! Here on the steep bridge over the river he found thrusting serpents, biting dogs and an ox that gored and fumed blocking the way. In the *Grímnismál* of the *Poetic Edda,* both the rivers Gjöll and the Leiptr wind through the world of man, but then fall to Hel.

FORGOTTEN WATERS: The Hidden Rivers of London

Indisputably, the Thames is the best known of London's rivers. Wending its way through the capital and beyond, it may surprise readers to learn that there is more to this influential waterway than meets the eye, and many hundreds of busy London commuters hurry by, little guessing at what lies beneath their feet. Numerous tributaries of the Thames that once flowed freely now run quietly beneath the bustling capital, driven underground one by one as the city expanded. Hidden they may be, but they are not lost: glimpses of these secret waterways are visible if you know but where to look.

These rivers have proved of great interest and inspiration to many over the centuries, from Victorian legends to Ben Aaronovitch's compelling Peter Grant series that features several of the lost rivers personified. Intriguingly, G.W. Lambert, in *The Geography of London Ghosts*, found that a significant number of supposed hauntings took place in properties close to buried rivers. Unsurprisingly, much folklore and many legends have grown up around these 'lost' rivers. Will you be intrigued enough to follow the old routes of these streams the next time you visit London?

Westbourne

In the 18th century, a section of this river was used to create the famous Serpentine at the behest of Queen Caroline, consort of George II. The spectacular 40-acre (16-ha) lake was created by damming up the selected area, only for the originating river to be cut off in 1834, the water considered too unsanitary to continue to supply the prestigious visitor attraction.

The Ranelagh sewer is a culvert of the Westbourne, created in the mid-19th century to hide the stench and filth of the river from more genteel eyes in the Sloane Square area of the city. Since the conversion, there have been enduring tales of ghostly sounds, leading to talk that the cellars of the houses are haunted. Of course, it is only the sound of the Westbourne, passing noisily through the pipes …

Crossing the Westbourne, Knights Bridge had a reputation for being a dangerous place to cross after dark, and one did so at one's peril. Another Westbourne crossing has the gory nickname of Bloody Bridge, not surprising given that the cook of Lord Harrington met his end there, beaten to death by highwaymen.

Tyburn

This evocatively named river conjures images of violence, death and bloody justice. The earliest written record of the Tyburn came in 785CE, however, and had much less macabre associations: the name comes from Teo Bourne, meaning 'boundary stream'.

Several well-known London locales once bore the name: Park Lane was once Tyburn Lane, and part of Oxford Street was Tyburn Road. These nods to the river have now vanished, but the legends prove more enduring. It is said that trees on the river's bank were used to hang criminals way back in the mists of time, but although it makes an appealing story, there is no evidence to support this. The infamous gallows of the same name was actually erected about 800m (half a mile) away in 1571, the location of Marble Arch today.

Today, the Tyburn still flows, running for part of its journey underneath Buckingham Palace. It can be glimpsed, however – if you believe the claims – flowing through the basement of Grays Antique Centre in Mayfair.

Fleet

Meaning a place where vessels can float, or that which is afloat, and perhaps the best known of London's lost rivers, the Fleet has given its name to both the street and the infamous prison. Incredibly filthy, and slated as such by Jonathan Swift in 1710, the river served as the primary sewer for the large number of mills and factories in the area, proving to be a very real health hazard to those in the locality.

A notorious inn on West Street that lay on the bank of the Fleet was the source of many dark tales. It was a most dissolute establishment indeed, run by a ruthless and terrible man: all manner of secret doors and trapdoors in the building allowed for murdered victims to be dispatched into the waters below, and also provided a handy means of escape for the thieves and other undesirables who congregated there. Unsurprisingly, such a location also gave rise to tales of ghostly goings-on.

The Fleet captured the imagination of that renowned observer of the Victorian underbelly of the capital: Charles Dickens. Fagin's den, where Oliver Twist had his first taste of crime, is said to have been based on the area the river flowed through.

All was not doom and gloom in the river's history: a selection of wells along the banks of the Fleet were believed to have the power to heal those who drank from them, earning the Fleet the name 'River of Wells'.

Walbrook

This Thames tributary was probably responsible for London's first water supply, and formed the western boundary of Roman Londinium. Indeed, it was on the east bank of this river that the Romans built a temple to Mithras in the mid-3rd century CE. There are different ideas on where the name came from, one suggested origin being the Anglo-Saxon for foreigner or stranger, due to the foreign trade seen by the river.

Although long since channelled underground, a hydrant was set off during the 1999 Carnival Against Capitalism, resulting in the Walbrook being set spectacularly free once more, for a time at least.

Effra

This south London river is one of the more outspoken of the capital's lost waterways, and has made its presence firmly felt throughout the centuries. There are several oft-repeated legends attached to the Effra, containing varying degrees of fact and fiction, as such tales do.

One of the more grisly is that of a coffin being dislodged from the nearby West Norwood cemetery by the periodic flooding of the Effra, working its way free with its gruesome load before finding its way out into the Thames. Although physically impossible given the dates for when this is said to have occurred and the history of the enclosing of the river, it was not unknown for coffins to move position in waterlogged ground, and it is possible this legend is indeed a mixture of fact and fiction.

Further back, in the 11th century, King Canute is said to have sailed up the Effra to Brixton, an enduring legend despite the width of the Effra and the size of the ships leaving this claim on shaky ground. Elizabeth I was also reputed to be a frequenter of the same waterway, sailing in her barge to visit Sir Walter Raleigh. A more recent urban legend has it that the wild tomatoes growing along the Effra's banks originated from the sewers, the seeds coming from the excrement of the more affluent tomato eaters in West London.

It is said that when the Effra was enclosed, the earth removed was used to build the banks of the Oval cricket ground.

Neckinger

Last but not least, the Neckinger, flowing from the long-demolished abbey at Bermondsey to the Thames, is one of the most enigmatic rivers on our list. The area through which the river flowed was one of the dirtiest and roughest of the capital, populated by slums, factories and asylums.

The word Neckinger comes from a bygone name for a neckcloth. The river is said to have a link with Satan himself, a map from 1740 labelling the wharf on the river as the Devil's Neckinger, an apt name indeed for it was there that pirates and assorted villains used to meet their end. In an interesting connection, the Devil's Neckinger was also a colloquial term for the noose. A less gory suggestion for the etymology of the river is that the name arose from the shape it made as it wended its way through the landscape.

A crossing point known as the Watering of St Thomas was a location for executions in the Tudor period. It was also mentioned by Chaucer as a watering place for horses *en route* to the shrine of Thomas Becket.

In yet another connection to death, in *Oliver Twist*, a branch of the Neckinger, Folly Ditch, was the location of the death of Bill Sikes.

WATERFALL FOLKLORE

Waterfalls churn with beauty and power, so it's unsurprising that many come with their own folklore. Niagara Falls, a group of three waterfalls on the border between Ontario, Canada, and New York state in the USA, is the site of the Indigenous tale: *The Maid of the Mist.*

The Maid of the Mist

This traditional story from the Haudenosaunee (also known as the 'Iroquois', though this is often seen as a derogatory exonym imposed on the group by colonialists) tells that the great Hé-no or Hinon – the spirit of thunder – made his home in a cave behind the veil of water, living there with his assistants who had been given to him by the Great Spirit. One year, a young maiden of Ga'-u-gwa village, above the falls, was betrothed to an old and disagreeable man. As the contract could not be broken, she committed to ending her life by throwing herself from the top of the waterfall. The girl took a great bark canoe, and went bravely to her death. Yet, seeing her fall, the god and his assistants caught the maiden in a blanket, and carried her to their cave behind the falls. Captivated by the girl's beauty, one of the assistants took her hand in marriage. Before this event, the village had been troubled by a great plague, and a year after the marriage the thunder spirit took pity on the girl. He whispered the secret of the illness to her, and the solution, and sent her into the village with this news.

It so happened that a giant snake lurked under the village. Each year, the snake would be overcome with an insatiable hunger, and would feast on the bodies of the dead buried near his lair. He would creep into the village and poison the water to ensure enough people would die to satisfy his hunger. Hé-no advised the people to move their homes to Buffalo Creek to escape the fiend. Yet the creature was intent on following his prey, and took to the waters, swimming with the current to find their new resting place. As he did, Hé-no sent out a great thunderbolt, which killed the monstrous snake. The creature's body floated downstream, blocking the waters when it stretched from one bank to the other until the land could resist no more. The gushing waters broke through, great chunks of land crumbling into the abyss below.

This is how the great Horseshoe Falls were born. Yet, should any curious wanderer seek to find the great Hé-no's dwelling place today, they will find nothing, for the cave also smashed into the churning waters, and was no more after the thunder god's great act of kindness for the people.

Controversially, a publicity poster by local artist Evelyn Carey, for the 1901 Pan-American Exposition in Buffalo, was released to over 35,000 postmasters across the country, depicting a scantily clad figure, veiled in French Art-Nouveau style. Entitled 'Spirit of Niagara', it is thought by some to be based on the Native American personification of the falls, or the maid from the tale of Hé-no. This would be seen as grossly inappropriate today, and an example of cultural appropriation of a traditional Indigenous story that many people still consider sacred.

A terrible phenomenon has been reported at the falls, whereby the brain sends the signal that one must step back – as the height is too much, and one might fall – yet this is often too quick to interpret correctly, and even today many people feel the urge to throw themselves to their death in the undulating waters below.

The Dragon's Gate

Waterfall lore also links to one of the most popular tattoo symbols: the koi fish of China. Koi fish tattoos are well-known symbols of courage and determination. Many people are unaware of the ancient story behind this symbol when they use it as a design – another example of how traditions can be appropriated by others across the world.

The tale tells that a school of koi were swimming up the Huang He, or Yellow River. Each tiny fish fought against the current, until they all – finally – reached the base of a great waterfall. Seeing the churning waters, many of the fish turned back, flowing downstream with the current. Yet a few of the golden school remained, determined to carry on their journey despite the obstacles. Jumping from deep in the depths of the waters, the koi used all their strength to try to reach the top of the waterfall, but with no success. Unbeknown to them, a group of demons sat in the undergrowth. Mocking and jeering, they used their demonic powers to make the waterfall even taller. The years passed until they became a century. And on this fateful day, one single golden koi managed to jump the great distance, and reach the top of the waterfall. As a reward for its determination, the gods gathered together and decided to honour the fish for its perseverance. The tiny fish was at once transformed into a great golden dragon, and its destiny was fulfilled.

This place has been named the Dragon Gate ever since, and while people generally attribute this tale to the waterfall in Hunan Province, many places with this name exist across China.

There is a Chinese proverb that goes: 'The carp has leapt through the dragon's gate', historically used when passing the exam to become part of the administration of the Chinese emperor. It now has a more general meaning: that if a person works diligently they will one day be rewarded with success.

Lover's Leap: Suicidal Lovers

The star-crossed lovers motif is a popular one throughout both folklore and literature, from Shakespeare's *Romeo and Juliet* to the tragic tale of 'The Dargle Lovers' who leapt to their deaths in County Wicklow, Ireland. Love – or lack of it – is a constant preoccupation of the human race, but sometimes it can take a dark turn.

The stunning setting of the Huay Kaew Waterfall in Thailand makes it a popular place for lovers to snatch a few moments together. According to legend, during the Second World War, a young woman named Bua Ban – beautiful, kindhearted, the loveliest in her village – fell in love with a soldier from Bangkok. He returned her affections, and the smitten lovers talked of marriage and the happy future they would spend together. When the soldier was called back to Bangkok, Bua Ban did not despair – her lover promised he would return, and they would be together.

Unfortunately for poor Bua Ban, the soldier was already married, and never intended to return, as he had reunited with his true wife. Expecting his child, heartbroken, shamed and alone, the jilted Bua Ban made her way up to the rocky precipice. Devoid of all hope, she threw herself to her death.

She is remembered in local legend in the name of the waterfall: the spot where she fell is known as Wang Bua Ban. It is believed that her spirit frequents the place, providing a place of pilgrimage for lovers hoping for a happier ending than Bua Ban herself. Intriguingly, another tale linked to the Huay Kaew falls tells of a rich young girl who fell in love with a boy beneath her station. Despite their deep attraction to each other, the girl's family forbade their union, arranging instead another match for their daughter. The ill-fated couple continued to meet in secret until the day before the wedding. In desperation, vowing never to be parted, the pair leapt from the top of the waterfall, cheating fate as they met their end together.

OBA'S EAR: A Tale of the Yoruba River Spirit

'Cry Me a River' is not just the title of a song, it's an idea that actually has parallels in West Africa. For the Yoruba people, orishas are multidimensional deities and spirits that represent the forces of nature: Oba is one of these. She is the Orisha of the River Oba, and one of the wives of Shango, a king of the Oyo Empire – also an orisha. While there are many versions of her story, one of the most popular tells of how a rival co-wife, Oshun, convinced Oba to serve up her very own ear as a meal for her husband, to show her love for him and gain his attention. This goes horribly wrong, as you might imagine, and ends with Shango banishing Oba from the house forever when he realizes she has mutilated herself. Some say that, in her grief, she cried enough tears to make the Oba River flow, while others say that she herself became the river that now flows through Iwo city in Nigeria. The churning rapids that appear where the river intersects with the Oshun River show the anger and rivalry between the two wives to this day.

This story of Oba and her ear is now part of Santería, an Afro-Caribbean tradition developed in 16th-century Cuba by enslaved Africans – specifically the Yoruba people from Nigeria and Benin, who carried their beliefs, traditions and sacred dances with them when they were torn from their homes and trafficked across the seas. They mixed these practices with the Roman Catholicism they were forced to adopt by their oppressors, and used Roman Catholic saints to represent each orisha – Oba is represented by St Catherine of Siena. These traditions include having priests and priestesses act as intermediaries between people and their deities, where possession trance is used to communicate with orishas and the ancestors. Animals are sacrificed in a humane manner: the blood is offered up to the orishas, while the meat is often eaten after the ceremony for sacrifices, births and marriages, yet never after sacrifices offered for deaths or healing.

THE TOP FIVE River Spirits from Around the World

I French Melusine

The tale of this French water nymph goes back centuries. The first literary version was written by Jean d'Arras at the end of the 14th century, based on old documents kept at the castle of Lusignan, near Poitiers – yet there are many versions throughout northern and eastern France, as well as Luxembourg. A popular version tells that a youth, Raymond of Poitiers, the son of a count, one day came upon a nymph at a sacred spring in the forest of Coulombiers. The nymph agreed to be his wife, with just a single request: that he should grant her the gift of as much land around the spring as could be covered by a stag's hide, where she could build a castle. The tale tells that this did indeed come to pass, and the castle was named Lusinia, after the nymph herself, becoming the very same castle mentioned in d'Arras' telling of her story.

There was one addendum to this request – that she could come to her castle each Saturday and be entirely undisturbed – or the lovers would be separated forever. Of course, the young man agreed. But, as happens with all promises, the pledge withered as the years went on. One day, Raymond went to the castle after an old clergyman asked about his wife. On finding all but a single door open, he looked through the keyhole. There stood Melusine in her bath, her lower body the tail of a monstrous fish or serpent. In his sorrow,

Raymond shared her secret. Melusine left him forever, yet promised to hover over the castle whenever a French king – or indeed any of her descendants – was near his death. It's said that her footprint was visible in the room where she leapt from the window in grief, but one of the last times she was heard was at the command that her castle should be pulled down, when she wailed and cried terribly.

2
Greek Naiades

The naiades were female nymphs of the freshwater rivers, streams and wells in Greek mythology. Many of these spirits had individual names and were associated with specific locations across the world. Worshipped by local cults who made sacrifices to them, people believed many could offer magical healing and cleansing through ritual bathing. They were often seen as vengeful and jealous spirits. A boisterous annual folk festival, celebrated centuries later, was rooted in the tragic myth of one particular Greek naiad and offers a lovely example of how a myth can inspire folk festivals and celebrations in later times. Herodotus tells us that Pallas was the naiad of Lake Tritonis – said to be in Libya in ancient times, but thought by some to be in Boeotia in Greece, or in the south of modern-day Tunisia. Pallas was the child of Triton, a river god and son of Poseidon. Triton raised the young Athena along with Pallas, and taught both girls the art of war. One day they took part in what some say was a mock battle, others a falling-out, hurling spears at one another. Zeus, loath to see Athena lose, distracted Pallas. The spear inflicted a mortal wound, and the naiad breathed her last. In her grief, Athena made a wooden statue of the girl, which became the famous Palladium stolen from Troy by Diomedes and taken to Rome by Aeneas.

It's said that this myth led to a festival celebrated in Libya to honour Athena. Herodotus tells us that the girls would be separated into two groups, then armed with stones and staves to fight each other. The crowd would choose their favourite before the event, and arm them with Corinthian helmets, put them in a chariot and carry them round the lake; any girls dying of their wounds would be given the title 'false virgins'. Charming.

3
Italian Anguane

In the national epic of the Ladin people from the Dolomites of north-eastern Italy – *The Rëgn de Fanes* ('Kingdom of Fanes') – the anguane are sacred lake nymphs who take human form, yet with near-transparent bodies. Helpful to humans, they can offer the gift of fertility and predict the future, often through prophetic dreams. Singing the sweetest songs, they live deep in lakes, or very close to them. They know the secrets of witches and can speak the language of owls. While not immortal, it's said they will live as long as the world lasts.

4
French Fenettes

In French mythology, fenettes are dangerous water fairies that come from the River Rhône, near Lake Geneva. The sweet, sad song of these evil fairies drifts through the reed-covered marshlands, soon becoming a gloomy groaning. It's said that

anyone working the land or fishing in the waters withdraws quickly, never turning to look at what pursues them, as sight of the fairies will lead to death within just a year.

5
Norwegian Fossegrim

The fossegrim is a male Norwegian river sprite, famous for playing the fiddle under waterfalls and in millponds. He often plays on dark evenings and will teach anyone who brings him an offering: the student must look away and throw a white kid into a north-flowing waterfall – but only on a Thursday. Grimm says a black lamb is another fitting sacrifice. A lean goat is enough to ensure the learner will be able to tune the instrument, yet a fat goat ensures that the fossegrim will grasp the learner's hand and use it to play the fiddle until the fingers bleed; after this tuition they will play so well even the trees will dance, and waterfalls will stand still.

THE MYSTERIOUS WATERS OF SCOTLAND

Scottish folklore is replete with all manner of strange and terrifying creatures lurking in its rivers and lakes. Perhaps even more disturbing, however, are the spirits reported to lie in wait to prey on the unwary.

The evocatively named shellycoat is one such spirit. As the name implies, a shellycoat's main identifying feature is the shells it wears, these adornments clattering together to make a loud and frightsome noise. Unlike some water spirits, the shellycoat isn't out for blood; the danger with this creature is the penchant it has for trickery and instilling fear into the hearts of unwary travellers for its own amusement. In one tale, two men fell victim to the questionable humour of a shellycoat. On the banks of the River Ettrick, they heard a cry; fearing that some unfortunate person had tumbled into the water and was now battling for survival, they hurried to their aid. It soon became apparent this would not be as easy as first anticipated; not only could they not locate anyone, but the voice moved away, going upriver. The two men followed the pitiful voice throughout the night, the futility of their mission becoming clear when, upon reaching the top of the mountain that the river climbed, instead of finding anyone, the voice started to descend again on the other side! It was, of course, none other than a shellycoat, his satisfied laughter filling their ears as they slunk off on their way.

What then of the boobrie? Said to frequent the highland lochs, the boobrie – or *tarbh boibhre* ('bull cow-giver') – is believed to take its name from its cow-like behaviour. As the belief goes, this

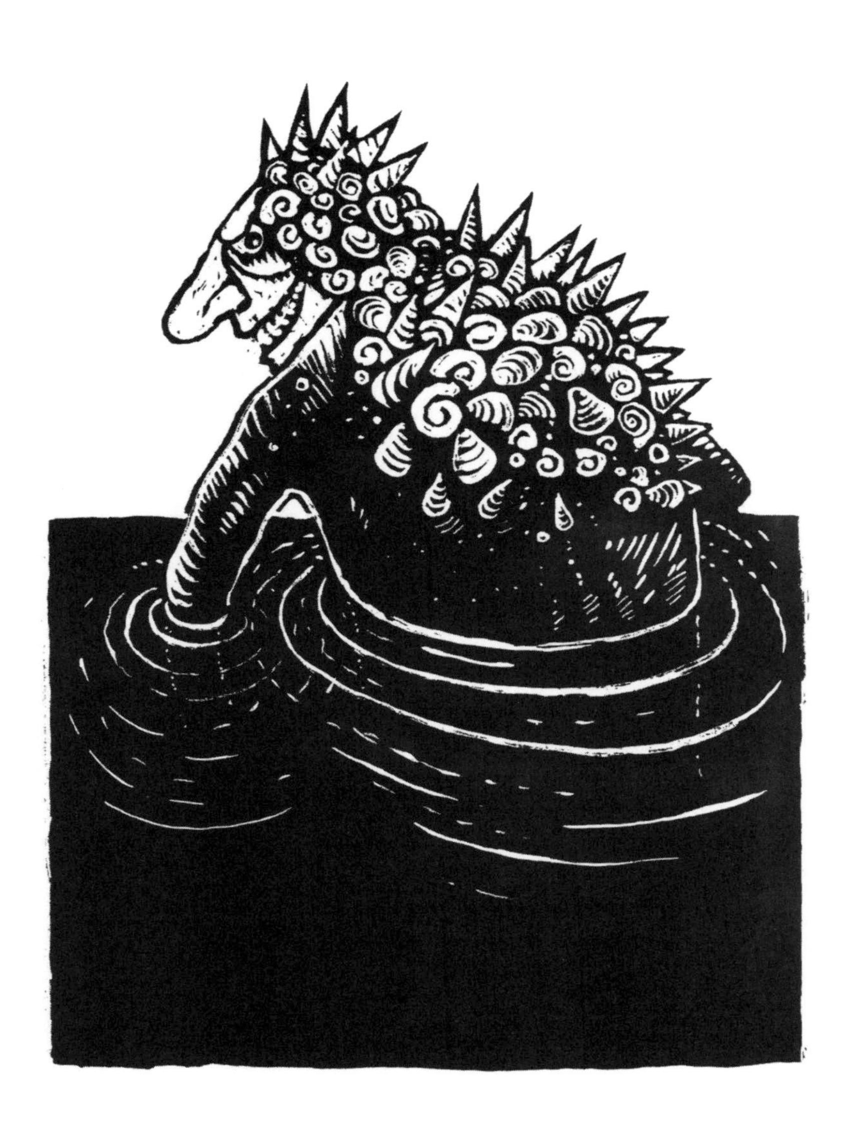

spirit wanted to join the cows that drank from the river, and so took on the appearance of a cow or bull to better achieve this aim. It could not entirely conceal its true nature, however; rather than sounding like a cow or bull, it made a noise like a terrifying bird.

Along with these two more common forms, the boobrie was also reported as a water horse, the *each-uisge*. Other forms it could take ranged from a large fly, a serpent bull and an earwig with a penchant for horse blood, the size of a man's little finger. It was believed to actually favour the shape of a bird, so terrible in appearance that it would have to be seen to be believed. This incarnation of the boobrie had a body larger than 17 eagles, a long sharp bill and huge claws on the end of webbed feet. The sound it made was just as terrible as its appearance – like a loud, enraged bull. This creature preyed on calves, lambs and sheep, and otters. The boobrie, in bull form at least, was thought to be not always evil. In one tale, it rescued a woman named Phemie from a rejected suitor who tried to carry her off; after knocking the man down, it took her to safety.

It is thought that the boobrie and ideas of its appearance come from sightings of the bird species the great auk. It is unlikely you would run into one of these creatures today; it was thought to have become extinct by the mid-19th century due to its habitat of heather being burned.

The *bean-nighe*, or the washerwoman at the ford, is believed to be a fairy or otherworldly woman. Found alone by ill-frequented rivers or streams, the bean-nighe is a terrible sight, washing, it is said, the clothes of those soon to die. She is best avoided, the sight of her serving as a death omen. This spirit doesn't cause harm herself, but seals the fate of others if not stopped. They are believed to be spirits of women who died giving birth, leaving life before their time. The bean-nighe is doomed to continue with her thankless task of washing until the day she would have left the earth.

The appearance of this spirit differs from area to area. In Perthshire, the bean-nighe is 'small and round' and wears green.

On the Isle of Skye, on the other hand, she is characterized as childlike and squat, small of stature. Other identifying features of the bean nighe are long dangling breasts. They are so long that she throws them over her shoulders to keep them out of the way, and it is this habit that can be the quick-thinking observer's salvation. If the discoverer can grab one and get it to his mouth to suckle, she becomes his nursing mother, and he her foster child. She will then tell him whatever he wants to know – including who is about to die. There were other ways to gain mastery over this ghostly washerwoman. In some areas, catching the bean-nighe at swordpoint meant she had to tell whoever caught her everything she knew. This could also mean on some occasions that her captor had to tell her everything she asked in return.

WATER HORSES: Majestic and Malevolent Creatures from the Depths

A lonely and weary traveller finds himself walking beside a river, when suddenly he hears the sound of something moving through the water. The beat of hooves, the flash of a mane, and then, there, a horse: the answer to all his woes. The man mounts without caution, but this is no ordinary steed. He has become the next victim of one of folklore's less friendly creatures: the water horse.

One of the most famous water horses is the Scottish kelpie. However, while the terms are often used interchangeably, water horses and kelpies are two distinct creatures in Scottish folklore, with the latter found in rivers, while water horses such as the each-uisge frequent the lakes and lochs.

With the unwary traveller on his back, the kelpie ultimately drags his victims down beneath the water to their death. There were ways to cheat the kelpie, however. In some tales it was possible for the kelpie to be at least seemingly tamed, made to do one's bidding by way of a bridle marked with a cross. This control would prove illusory and fleeting, and the moment the work was done the kelpie would flee back to its watery home, sometimes taking the rider with it. In one story, we learn that it is possible to kill a kelpie, the deed on this occasion carried out using that scourge of so many folkloric creatures: red-hot iron.

The prominence of the kelpie in Scottish folklore is evident from the sculptures located near Falkirk and visible from the M9 motorway. Measuring a staggering 30m (98ft) tall, they have been part of the landscape since 2013, testament to the enduring hold the kelpie has over the Scottish imagination. Another testament to the lasting and far-reaching nature of the legend is the appearance of the kelpie in modern literature, such as the works of Lari Don and an entry in J.K. Rowling's *Fantastic Beasts and Where to Find Them.*

Despite this great fame, interestingly, the kelpie or indeed any variant is not present south of the border in English folklore, with England's lakes and rivers being decidedly lacking in water horses of any kind.

This deficit is redressed in Wales where there are tales of the Ceffyl Dŵr. Still a staple of Welsh folkloric belief into the 19th century, the Ceffyl Dŵr varied in appearance and purpose. In the north of the country, the horse was just one form taken by this spirit that was prone to shapeshifting and violence towards people. In the south, the Ceffyl Dŵr presented consistently as a small horse, enchanting in appearance, that lured people onto its back. Speed is commonly remarked upon in tales of the Ceffyl Dŵr, and they are said to be able to cover huge distances in an impossibly short space of time before vanishing, leaving the hapless rider to drown. One exception to this rule – and an example of denominational equality – was where clergymen were concerned. Clergymen of any creed were said to be able to ride the horse without the rude treatment afforded to others, and there are several tales that relate how a minister reached his destination unscathed, while their accompanying clerk or deacon were left behind or thrown into the water.

The Scandinavian water horse is the *bäckahäst* or 'brook horse'. Most often seen when foggy, the bäckahäst is described as a majestic and luminous being. After beguiling riders into mounting, it plunges back down beneath the water to drown the victim, who is unable to dismount. Frequently in tales of the bäckahäst, those who ride the animal are children, perhaps because they are deemed more foolhardy, or perhaps to increase the sense of peril and impending tragedy in the reader. One popular version

is that of a group of boys playing on a winter evening near a frozen river. When a beautiful horse appears, they climb onto it one by one. The last child, marvelling at the sight of his friends all mounted, declares the horse to be amazing, using a colloquial phrase that also happens to rhyme with the words Jesus Christ, which he says instead due to mispronunciation. The horse then disappears, leaving the lads with sore behinds but saved, due to the bäckahäst's hatred of the name of Christ. Despite the terrible predictions, many, or in fact most, tales end with the riders surviving. Like the kelpie, the bäckahäst could also, according to some tales, be put to work, sometimes because the rider had tricked it.

HUMPED SERPENTS AND VICIOUS EELS: Loch Ness and the World's Most Fearsome Lake Monsters

There is something undeniably compelling about tales of large monsters lurking in the depths of lakes and rivers. Although each individual monster, or type of monster, is firmly rooted in the location associated with it, it might be surprising to note that sightings of such creatures share certain characteristics across different places, times and locations. The reliable, upstanding nature of witnesses cited, the appearance of the monsters themselves – often described as 'humped', or in other cases eel- or serpent-like – and attempts in recent years to photograph the creatures have been key in the development of such tales, further fuelling debate and the continuation of the legends. Here are a few of the most fascinating lake monsters across the world.

Although it is impossible to know when the oral tradition of a monster in Loch Ness began, An Niseag – or the Loch Ness Monster as it is more famously known – first entered the historical record in written form in the 6th century. In the *Life of St Columba*, a man is tragically killed by a water beast or monster while out on the River Ness, and the saint successfully saves one of his own companions from the same fate by compelling it to back off in the name of God. There is some dispute as to whether this describes the same creature that in the 20th century became known as Nessie. A 12th-century manuscript by Walter

of Bingham, held by the British Library, actually depicts the monster as a large bear-like creature. Despite occasional sightings of something in the loch, they were few and far between until an account by George Spicer was published in the *Inverness Courier* in 1933. According to Spicer, a creature about 12m (40ft) long with a long neck crossed the road in front of his car, before entering the nearby loch. This sparked a spate of further sightings and reports, and the interest in Nessie remains until this day.

In Lake Lagarfljót in Iceland, a large worm of the same name is said to lurk beneath the waters. Another monster with a long pedigree, it is suggested that the first mention of the Lagarfljót Worm is from the 14th century, when in 1345 a 'wonderful thing' was recorded in the Icelandic annals. No head or tail was seen, but humps were witnessed rising out of the water. Further tantalizing detail is provided in a map from 1585, where the intriguing 'in this lake appears a large serpent' is engraved beside the lake itself. The 'worm' has been witnessed across the centuries that followed, and it is said to be up to 12m (40ft) long. Most popular explanations for these sightings include misidentification of foam floating on the water, bubbles of methane gas, and debris from a nearby forest and mountain.

The horse-headed, serpentesque inkanyamba of South Africa has its origins in both Zulu and Xhosa beliefs and folklore. Said to eat the bodies of those who fall into the water, and to attack those who come too close, this name is given to a group of creatures, though the most famous is the one said to reside in KwaNogqaza (the Place of the Tall One) at Howick Falls, in KwaZulu-Natal Province. These creatures have a wide span of operations, with sightings occurring in several other locations, including the Mkomazi River, nearly 72km (45 miles) away from Howick. Meaning 'tornado' in the Zulu language, the inkanyamba are blamed for violent storms over the summer, a belief also reflected in the Xhosa idea that the creatures take to the skies during those months in order to mate. In the late 20th century journalists recorded a belief among locals that a tornado that struck the village of Impendle was a huge snake. Storms that led to 2,000 people losing their homes were also blamed on the creature's wrath. There continued to be regular sightings, and a reward was offered in 1995 for photographic evidence of the creatures. Unfortunately, the only picture to result was proven to be a hoax. It is believed by many that inkanyamba are actually a form of eel – large, carnivorous and migratory, but not the monsters of legend.

The Banyoles monster was a terrible, dragon-like creature found in Banyoles Lake in Girona, northern Spain. During the 8th century, this dragon struck terror into locals with its penchant for feasting on livestock and people alike. According to the legend, the most powerful army belonging to Charlemagne came to vanquish the beast, but the soldiers' confidence proved misplaced: the army was decimated, the people left more hopeless than ever. Could no one save them? In desperation, some of the villagers visited France, where they sought the advice of a monk, St Emeterio. He drew the creature from the watery depths with prayers and words, and in doing so, either turned it into a peaceful creature, or – according to some versions – discovered that it already was, and that the rumours of its terrible deeds were merely a cover story for the pillaging army. Whichever version you believe, some say the Banyoles monster is still to be found in the lake to this day, where it lives peacefully enjoying a vegetarian diet!

Ogopogo

Canada boasts several lake monsters to its name, one of the most famous being the Ogopogo, purported to live in the Okanagan Lake, British Columbia. This legendary 'monster' has gained local popularity and fame: as the subject of a film, and depicted by several statues, a postage stamp, and even as the logo for a British Columbian hockey team, the Kelowna Rockets. It was even said to have been caught on camera when film footage claiming to be of Ogopogo was captured by Art Folden in 1968. This was analyzed and debunked in 2005 by Benjamin Radford; although it shows a creature, it is either a beaver or bird.

However, this popular creature is more controversial than it appears. Some believe that this 'monster' was originally the spirit of the lake in First Nations' tradition, known as N'ha-a-itk in the Salish language, only later turning into the monster people recognize today when outsiders moved into the area and reimagined the spirit into a physical creature. It's said that the name Ogopogo was only introduced as recently as 1924, with an old London music-hall song about the monster performed at the Vernon Rotary Club in the northern Okanagan Valley. Some reports tell that in its original form, the N'ha-a-itk or Naitaka spirit was paid a live tribute of chickens and other small creatures that were killed and then dropped into the lake to guarantee safe passage through the water.

While not many know of the water spirit today, it still lives on: at the 1992 Salish Conference, a Shuswap (Secwépemc) participant did indeed say that he had been told by elders that there was a large snake in a local lake. It's been said by some that Ogopogo, the so-called 'lake monster', probably does have firm origins in sacred Okanagan cosmology.

Folklore or Fakelore? The Monster of Bear Lake

Situated on the border of Utah and Idaho in the USA, Bear Lake is said to be home to a strange creature of its own. In 1868, Joseph C. Rich, a Mormon from the area, printed a piece in the *Deseret News* that was to grip the imagination of all and sundry. There was, according to Rich, an old Native American story of a large, serpent-like creature that lurked beneath the waters of Bear Lake. Not only that, but this monstrous beast had been witnessed in recent times by several settlers in the region.

In the wake of the initial sightings, the area was gripped with monster fever. Between them, witnesses described a creature between 12 and 27m (40 and 90ft) long, with large eyes about 30cm (12in) apart, whose ears were bunch-like on the side of its head. Descriptions of the head itself varied, with some saying it was like a cow, while others likened it to a crocodile. Another description was of a tuskless walrus. Despite no one having seen the underside of it, it was also said that the beast moved clumsily on land, but more than made up for that in the water where it moved at great speeds, up to 100km/h (60mph) according to some observers. Many of those that had sighted the creature were reliable, upstanding members of the community, this fact lending weight to the story.

No doubt in response to its new-found celebrity, leaving its initial location, the monster – or one like it – was sighted in other lakes. As the tale grew, there were also claims of a second creature – potentially a mate – and even small, young monsters. It was said that everyone in the region believed in the existence of this creature.

Interest in the story finally ran its course, and after a few years mentions in the newspapers dwindled. There were those who were sceptical from the outset, notably competing newspapers, and 26 years after the initial article, Rich himself finally admitted to having fabricated the story. Widely accepted as 'fakelore', this does little to detract today from interest in the infamous lake monster. A quick trawl of comments on internet articles reveals many who claim belief in the creature, and even those who insist they have seen it for themselves.

The Bear Lake Monster has also made its way into fiction, in the tales of cowboy Pecos Bill. The exploits of this hero of the Wild West were created by Edward O'Reilly and published in *Century Magazine* in 1923, and included such daring deeds as lassoing a twister or cyclone. He was also said to have made a bet that he could wrestle the great Bear Lake Monster into submission. Pecos Bill did just that and, in a beautiful example of how folklore transcends cultural and geographical bounds, he flung the much-feared creature so hard and far that it landed in Scotland in Loch Ness, becoming the lake monster so many look for today!

THE FOLKLORE OF SWAMPS AND MARSHES

Not far from New Orleans, in the swamps of Slidell, Louisiana, there's said to be a monster lurking in the woodlands. Two men, Billy Mills and Harlan Ford, are the first people who claimed to witness the creature in 1963, and said they managed to make a cast of its tracks a decade on. Years later Dana Holyfield, Ford's granddaughter, unearthed alleged footage of the creature, supposedly filmed in the 1970s, featured on Fox News. Now named the Honey Island Swamp Monster, it's said to be a hairy, human-like creature, over 2m (6½ft) high. Online videos and reports with people claiming to have witnessed the monster in recent years abound. Dana Holyfield herself has produced a film documenting the creature and collecting accounts to prove the veracity of her grandfather's story and honour his memory. In a filmed interview another eyewitness, Ted Williams, claimed he saw the creature jump a bayou and watched two of the monsters swimming in a river, stating that they looked human but with arms hanging by their knees. In another recent siting Herman Broom remembered it had a 'face like a man, and a body like an animal'.

Yet monsters that lurk in the Louisiana swamps are not just a modern phenomena. The Létiche is the soul of an unbaptized child that swims in the bayous of Terrebonne Parish, blamed for unsettling the *pirogues* (tree-trunk canoes) that navigate the waterways. Some say that this is a creature from Houma (Native American) legends, and the origin of the Cajun loup-garou. Similar to the European werewolf, the loup-garou is a human-wolf hybrid cursed to drink human blood. The only way to combat the creature is to throw salt over it, at which it will promptly turn to dust.

In Indigenous Australian beliefs, particularly from the Kulin nations and the area around Victoria – still living traditions today – the fearsome bunyip haunts creeks and billabongs. Sometimes said to be a devil or a dreaded water spirit, eyewitness accounts from the Barwon lakes near Geelong in 1845 say it is over 3.5m (11½ft) tall, sporting an emu-like head with a serrated beak, and the body and legs of an alligator. It has a brightly feathered chest, gigantic claws and lays large blue eggs double the size of those belonging to an emu. It is amphibious, swimming frog-like, and only ventures onto the bank to bask on hot days. It walks upright on its hind legs and kills by hugging people to death. Further reports come from William Buckley, a Cheshire man who lived with the Wathaurong people between 1803 and 1835, who described it as having grey feathers, and being the size of a calf. He said bunyip only venture from the water when the weather is calm, and they have a supernatural power to cause illness and even death. One sign of a bunyip in the lagoon is a massive amount of eels; it's believed that they are specifically there because of the bunyip's presence, for him to feast on. It's thought that the creatures are viewed as supernatural by Indigenous Australians, and anyone killing a bunyip might even forfeit their own life.

Wherever you are in the world, when walking near stagnant waters, remember that they have lain in the land, long undisturbed … and who knows what might be lurking in the depths.

Sinister Bog Lights: Will-o'-the-Wisp

The road is long and the traveller weary, though he is not yet near his destination. Suddenly, in the distance, he spots a light, glowing and beckoning, urging him to follow. Thinking it might be a short-cut, some kind soul showing him the way, he steps from the path, deciding it is worth the risk. It is a choice that he might well live to regret, if he is lucky – as the traveller ventures onto the increasingly marshy land, the solid ground he has left so rashly no longer visible, the light is the only thing that can be identified for certain in the gloom. Still optimistic, he continues on, and on, growing wearier with each moment. Suddenly, without warning, the light goes out, just as the traveller feels his foot sink into the water …

That water has posed a danger to travellers across the millennia is indisputable, this very fact is made glaringly apparent by the large number of legends focused on this most treacherous of nature's elements. *Ignis fatuus* – fool's fire – exists in many variations in folklore across the world. Witnessed especially over swamps, marshes and bogs, these atmospheric lights are particularly prevalent across Europe, Norway and areas of the USA. Presenting in varying hues and sizes, these lights are frequently said to lure travellers to a watery fate or, at best, leave them hopelessly lost.

In England, the common name for such lights is will-o'-the-wisp. Derived from 'wisp', the 17th-century word meaning a bundle of hay or straw, and is often said to be someone called Will holding a lighted torch. Will's American counterpart is Jack-o'-lantern, and both are frequently depicted as having malicious or mischievous intent, and these lights are often referred to as spook lights, orbs or ghost lights.

Within European folklore, there are many explanations for these intriguing lights. Some say they are linked to the fairies. Others believe a man named Will or Jack, doomed to haunt the watery marshlands for all eternity due to some terrible deed committed during life, is the source of the lights that bob and dance in the distance. According to Swedish folklore, the lights are the souls of those who have died unbaptized. Ever hopeful, they lead travellers to the water in the hope that they themselves can receive the sacrament of baptism that they missed in life.

The Bengali phenomenon of Aleya – 'marsh ghost light' – appears to fishermen, causing confusion and leading to them becoming lost, sometimes forever, drowned in the marshes. Traditions in West Bengal and Bangladesh hold that the lights are the ghosts of fishermen who lost their lives at their work. They are not always intent on harm, however, some actually leading people away from danger, to escape the fate they met themselves.

The Hessdalen of Norway, Marfa Lights of Texas, and Hobby Lantern of Europe to name but a few, known by different names in different places ... the descriptions of these ghostly lights are intriguingly similar, descriptions across time and place being startlingly consistent.

In the Scottish highlands, the ghostly lights, known as Spunkie, are common around lochs and have a more human form. Resembling a link boy (children who would illuminate the way for pedestrians with a lighted torch), the Spunkie was well-known for leading those who followed him to a deadly end. There was no end to the mischief caused by this manifestation, also causing ships to be wrecked by luring them onto the rocks, thinking it to be light of the harbour.

In the West Country of England, in Cornwall and Devon, such spirits are known as pixy-light: they are responsible for luring travellers into the dangerous bogs of the area. The swamp-ridden Massachusetts' Bridgewater Triangle in the USA has a history of sightings of ghostly lights. These are not just an historic occurence however – modern sightings are equally plentiful.

Scientific theories to explain these lights have abounded since at least the 16th century, when the lights were attributed to the decay of organic matter. Today, the accepted explanation is that the lights are caused by the oxidation of phosphine, diphosphine and methane.

There is also considerable lore that the lights mark the location of treasure: in Finland, St John's Day was the time to look, as the lights would reveal the location of riches hidden by others.

THE SHAPESHIFTING PINK DOLPHIN OF THE AMAZON RIVER

In Brazil, accounts of the infamous Boto Encantado – or enchanted dolphin – occur as early as the 19th century. As large as a canoe, they swim incredibly fast and move between animal and human form at will. Reputedly shameless creatures that enjoy dancing at parties, they enter houses silently at night to paralyze their victims before taking advantage of them. These creatures seduce unsuspecting women with their passionate embrace, and sire numerous illegitimate children – there are even cases where mothers have legally listed the father of their child as just such a dolphin. Many women are often left bewildered when their Romeo rushes off, dives into the river and swims away after their rendezvous; while others remember nothing afterwards, the visits only becoming apparent when they grow pale and thin after repeated encounters. In contrast, the female botos are so insatiable that the only way to stop a man engaging with her is to hit him smartly on the leg. Looking into the eyes of such a dolphin – *maulhado de bicho* (the creature's evil eye) – can cause a type of madness, where the afflicted try again and again to jump into the river, as they alone can hear the dolphins calling to them. Despite their reputation, anyone who kills a pink dolphin will be punished with a curse: they can never catch food again, and only a *curador* – a healer – can lift the affliction. Today, the Worldwide Fund for Nature is attempting to tag and study river dolphins throughout Bolivia, Brazil and Columbia, since they are under threat of disappearance due to pollution of their natural habitat; they are classified as 'vulnerable' in some areas.

BE CAREFUL WHERE YOU REST: The Insatiable Appetite of the Irish Joint Eater

Be very wary indeed if you happen to fall asleep beside a stream. For it is then that the Irish *alp-luachra* – or joint eater – is said to strike. This small, newt-like creature is in reality a bad fairy, a parasite that preys on the slumbering walker or traveller. Slipping unseen down their throat, it sets up camp in the stomach, stealing any food consumed until the victim wastes away and perishes from sheer starvation as loved ones look on helplessly. How to fight the unseen enemy? Some say they can be drawn out by the smell of strong food. They may also reveal themselves if the host eats something salty, then waits by a stream for them to abandon their host in search of water.

Although a very sneaky foe, there are signs that can reveal the parasitical creature. Pain and a huge, insatiable appetite are said to betray the presence of the joint eater, while the victim wastes away even as he gorges himself. While tales of the joint eater are many, perhaps the most sensational of all is that of the man who had a grand total of 13 of these parasitical creatures within him – thankfully, due to the help of a beggar man and a prince, he lived to tell the tale!

Despite their ghastly reputation, these creatures are not all bad; licking an alp-luachra is said to be a good cure for burns.

WELL FOLKLORE

Wells have been used as a source of life-giving water across the world since prehistory, so it's no surprise that myths, tales and legends surrounding them abound in many cultures. They are seen as a source of wisdom, used to highlight stupidity; they are places of deep mystery and unrivalled horrors. At the bottom of the wells in Malta lurk unspeakable terrors: the *belliegña*, which snatches away unsuspecting children and has the power to make wells dry up or overflow; and the *mñalla*, a giant eel that lurks in the depths and preys on anyone who ventures into its lair.

Wells are often sacred places, with deities, saints or spirits associated with them. In India, *năgas* are a semi-divine race who are half-human and half-cobra. These beings can shapeshift to either appear as entirely human, or in snake form, sometimes with many heads. Banished to live underground by Brahma, and ordered to only bite truly evil people, the năgas often reside in wells, lakes and rivers, and are guardians of treasure or doorways; statues of them are often found watching over the entrances of temples. In a contemporary twist to the use of traditional stories in the modern-day media, a public row ensued over 'racist revisionism' after a South Korean actress was cast to play Nagini in the movie *Fantastic Beasts: Crimes of Grindelwald* – a cursed Asian female character subservient to the white, male Voldemort. People complained further when J.K. Rowling made an error on Twitter: that *năgas* are originally from Indonesian mythology, rather than Hindu.

Well dressing is a tradition practiced throughout Staffordshire and Derbyshire in England, thought to date back to at least the 18th century. Wells are decorated with flowered panels, often depicting scenes from the Bible, from May to September by local children and community groups. The most famous site for the custom is Tissington in Derbyshire, which some say developed to give thanks for the village being spared from plague in the 14th century due to the waters being so pure, while others believe it's a remnant of ancient practices to honour water spirits. Clootie wells are places of pilgrimage in many Celtic areas, found across Wales, Scotland, Cornwall and Ireland. Munlochy, on the Black Isle in Scotland, is one of the best examples of these wells. Believed to be the site of an ancient church, the remaining spring is dedicated to St Curidan, where sick and disabled children were once left overnight for healing. Here, to this day, strips of cloth called clooties are submerged in the sacred waters, then tied to a nearby tree with a prayer or wish whispered with each ribbon, in the belief or hope they will come to fruition as the cloth disintegrates. Some groups are now trying to raise awareness around such practices due to environmental concerns. They aim to encourage people to only tie clooties made from natural fibres, as cloth containing plastic will never decay. Not only does this mean the folk magic won't work, but it means that the items will remain forever – or at least until someone clears them away. Some have labelled these kinds of offerings 'ritual litter' and are trying to raise awareness of practicing responsible folk magic and rituals in the modern day.

Similar customs are observed in France, for instance at Courbefy, where offerings like coins and flowers are left in the area at three wells dedicated to St Eutrope. *Ex-voto* offerings to ask God for his grace and healing are also given; this type of offering is usually either a strip of cloth, shoe or piece of clothing that has been in contact with the patient's body, providing a magical link to the owner. Yet the most famous curative spring in France has to be that at Lourdes, where it's said that 70 miraculous cures were reported out of the 555 sick who attended in 1879, while this figure doubled the following year. An estimated 2–4 million pilgrims flock for healing each year today.

In Norse mythology, the Well of Urðr is the well of fate that lies beneath the World Tree. From this well come the Norns, three maidens who dictate the fates of humanity and set their laws. Said

to represent the past, the present and the future, they are similar to other depictions of the three Fates or Destinies around the world, like the Greek Moirai or Graeae. Other examples include the Sudjenice or Narucnici of Croatian and Bulgarian folklore, who either appear as white maidens or as tall, cheerful old hags shrouded in white veils. Urðr is just one of three wells that lie in the roots of the World Tree: another is Hvergelmir, a bubbling, boiling spring; and the last is called the well of Mímir, guarded by the mysterious Mímir himself – said to be either an Aesir god or a giant. One shadowy tale from Norse myth tells that Odin once ventured into the depths of the World Tree, following the root that led to the realm of the giants. Here, beneath the root, he came to Mímir's Well. He asked for a drink from the waters, in order to gain knowledge of his fate. Mímir refused until the god offered to sacrifice his eye in return. This is how the infamous Allfather of the Norse gods came to have only one eye.

Yet not all well folklore is so profound. The infamous Nasreddin Hodja (or Nasreddin the Teacher) is a 13th-century trickster figure known throughout the Islamic world. He has an interesting encounter with a well in the darkly comic Turkish tale 'Restoring the Moon'.

One night, Hodja went to draw water from the well, but on looking down, saw the face of the moon staring right back up at him – it had obviously fallen into the well! Alarmed, he took a rope and hook to pull it back up. Yet the hook, catching on a rock, snapped as he pulled and pulled, making him stumble and injure himself. Lying flat on his back, Hodja noticed the moon sitting back in its sky. Relieved that his efforts hadn't been in vain, and that he had indeed pulled the moon from the well, he exclaimed, 'O praise and glory, I have suffered much pain, but the moon has got to its place again.'

A tale from Tibet (China) tells of a troop of monkeys with a similar plight, and in this case the leader of the group decided that they should form a chain of monkeys in order to pull the moon from the well – and so they did. Yet, as the monkeys reached and stretched, the branch that they clung to bent and bent, and soon the water became troubled; the branch promptly broke, and the monkeys fell about in a heap. A deity adds a moral to the tale, with the words: 'When the foolish have a foolish leader, they all go to ruin, like the monkeys which wanted to draw the moon up from the well.' A later story can be found in the controversial *Nights with Uncle Remus: Myths and Legends of the Old Plantation*, where Br'er Rabbit and his friends also try to retrieve the moon from a mill pond, to no avail. The tale ends with a little wisdom: You can only catch the moon in the millpond when you use fools for bait!

Strangely, folk tales from the UK mirror these stories. In West Yorkshire, it's said that a bunch of smugglers were caught in the act by the local militia. Loath to be punished for their misdeeds, the men declared that they were attempting to catch the moon from the water. Realizing that the men were talking about the moon's reflection, and concluding they must be a ha'penny short of a shilling, the law enforcement officers laughed, told them to carry on, and went on their way – leaving the men free to carry on their crimes. After this, 'moonraking' passed into local folk language, used to mean smuggling goods. The story is celebrated with the biennial Moonraking Festival in Slaithwaite, West Yorkshire, where locals make lanterns from willow and paper. The festival ends with floating a giant moon down the Huddersfield Narrow Canal on a raft, where – of course – people try to grab it with rakes, after which gnomes in beards rescue it, and parade it round the town, as one might expect! An almost identical tale was recorded in 18th-century Wiltshire in the south of England.

THE FOUNTAIN OF YOUTH

Given the human preoccupation with life and death, the fact that stories exist of waters that defy age and even death itself is to be expected. Today, the Budapest thermal springs are visited frequently for their medicinal and health benefits, while Lake Assal, a salt lake with healing properties in the Danakil Desert of north-east Ethiopia, southern Eritrea, and north-western Djibouti is well known for curing aching muscles and more joint problems. The most well-known throughout folklore and legend is that known as the fountain of youth. These waters take several different forms, variously an actual fountain, river or a spring. The idea is always the same, however: those that bathe in or drink the water have many years stripped from them and regain their youth.

The tale has a long vintage. Although not named specifically, Herodotus, writing in the 5th century BCE, tells of a fountain with magical properties. The King of the Macrobians told of how the minimum age his people lived to was a staggering 120 years. The source of such longevity was the violet-scented waters of the fountain, which left the skin smooth and restored.

Some say that the first origins of the story come from Eurasia, with the 13th-century Arabic *Romance of Alexander the Great* being one of the earliest written versions. In this story, Alexander looks on amazed as aged warriors pass through the waters, each emerging 30 years old again. Even more amazingly, men of over 100 years of age bathed there, only to leave the water as youths.

Legend has also linked the fountain with the exploratory voyages of Spaniard Ponce de León, who became Puerto Rico's first governor in 1509. According to the tale, the primary aim of his famed expedition of 1513 was to discover the location of the fountain of youth. However, there is no evidence in the historical record to support the search for the fountain as the main – or indeed any – aim of the voyage. Lack of proof does little to dampen the fervour of legend, however. The Fountain of Youth Archaeological Park, the place in modern-day Florida where Ponce de León was said to have first landed, was established in the mid-19th century, and tales of the fountain continue to excite and entice people even today.

MYTH AND MYSTERY: The Lady of the Lake

Arthur, that valiant king, noble warrior, had been lucky to escape his last battle with his life. Merlin had put his foe – the tallest knight in the entire land – into an enchanted sleep, and had taken Arthur to have his wounds healed by a skilled hermit. Now physically recovered, the King rode onwards with the wily sorcerer, lamenting his lack of a sword.

'Have patience,' Merlin cautioned, and he was again proved right. As they approached a large lake, an intriguing sight caught Arthur's eye. Out in the glistening water was a mysterious arm, holding aloft a beautiful sword.

'Who is that?' Arthur demanded.

'The Lady of the Lake,' Merlin responded. 'If you wish for the sword to be yours, you must ask her for it – be sure, however, to do so courteously.'
As if sensing his intent, the beautiful woman was gliding towards him over the water, and, as she approached, Arthur seized his chance.

'Who does the sword belong to?' he asked, adding

that he had lost his own weapon in battle.

'It is mine,' she replied, 'but I will gift it to you in return for something I will ask you for.'
Arthur agreed, and duly followed her instruction to enter the nearby barge, rowing it towards the sword. He took it with him, not forgetting her injunction to make sure not to leave the scabbard behind. It was the scabbard, Merlin later told him, that was most important, as he would never be injured whilst wearing it.

Viviane, Nimue, Nyneve. Whichever of the various names she is known by, the Lady of the Lake is inextricably connected with that most famous and legendary of English kings: Arthur. Credited with giving the great warrior his famed sword Excalibur, she has exerted a pull on the imaginations of artists, poets and authors across the centuries, and remains a vital character in retellings of the Arthurian tales today.

Aside from her pivotal role in Arthur's destiny, the Lady of the Lake has strong connections with two other prominent figures. According to some tellings, she enchanted Merlin, first by her physical beauty, and then, making it a condition of her capitulation, by the very magic she persuaded him to teach her. Utterly taken with her, Merlin wanted her for his own. The lady, however, had other ideas; she would only acquiesce if Merlin first taught her everything he knew, in effect making her as powerful as he was himself. The smitten sorcerer agreed, despite seeing only too well the fate that would befall him – eternal imprisonment in either a cave or tree.

The other important role played by this mysterious lady is that of fairy or foster-mother figure to Lancelot. Chrétien de Troyes, creator of this favourite knight, has him raised by a fairy in the lake. There is, however, potentially an even older German version with Lancelot raised on an island of thousands of happy maidens after being taken away by a merfeine or water fairy.

Just who was she? Some sources conflate her with Morgan le Fay, Arthur's sister, while another idea is that she was a third child to Uther Pendragon, sister to Arthur and Morgan. There is some argument that she was literally created from Merlin. In that subtle blend and development of language, the Welsh *hwimleian chwyfleian* – meaning a pale-faced wanderer – is said to have been corrupted into 'Viviane' in the French telling of Arthur and his knights. Originally meaning Merlin himself, this morphed into a fair maiden, and over time the mysterious and ethereal lady who entrapped Merlin was born and adopted into the Arthurian canon.

CONCLUSION: What Can We Learn from Our Seas and Rivers?

Seascapes, and the rivers and pools that go hand-in-hand with them, are just one part of the landscape of the wondrous planet we live on. When the ideas for this book were still forming, fresh and full of possibilities, we were inspired to create something that uncovered a profound truth about humanity – for that is what folklore is inherently about, after all.

Our myths, legends and folk tales hold age-old wisdom. This learning has been gathered over centuries and encoded into symbols, archetypes and stories that make those truths of life easier to understand. Thus it is easier to remember and pass on this information with a mere tale, to anyone who might wish to listen.

Our customs, beliefs and traditions show our reverence of nature and its spirits, and we use these rites and rituals to breathe meaning into the world in which we live. We use them to mark important events in life, to show how times like the birth of a child, or the joining of two people in marriage, are different and special events. Our mourning rituals help us to grieve and heal. No matter who we are, or where we are from, we all have ways of mourning, our ways of welcoming life.

In this book, we have seen many stories, many rituals. We have seen how these customs vary greatly from place to place across the world. Yet, we have also seen how they come inherently from the same place within ourselves as humans: we have seen offerings given over to the seas and rivers for the protection of our loved ones when fishing and travelling the great watery expanses of the globe.

We have looked upon the face of the spirits of our waters, and while they might look different – from Mami Wata to Poseidon, from the fossegrim to the naiads – their role in our lives is the same. They aid us when we are lost. They offer us healing. We plead and bargain with them for their gifts and blessings. Humans everywhere look to the water and see the possibilities it holds in its depths. It is cathartic, cleansing and majestic, with a power to consume all; a regenerative force that ebbs and flows like time, with the power to give life or take it away.

We have seen, on our journey, our inherent human fear of the unknown: personified in the Kraken, the Loch Ness Monster, and the inkanyamba alike. Across the world we create the devils of the deep to warn children – all children from all places – from straying too close to the edge. For we know only too well to be wary of the depths, filled with death and danger for land creatures such as ourselves, irrespective of whether we are from the mountains, the deserts or the coastal plains. Water embodies both our fears and our dreams.

In this journey through the stories and traditions of the rivers and seas of the world, we have seen tales of sacred rivers and the threat of pollution that they face. We have seen that the fate of legendary river dolphins across the world – from India to Brazil – lies within our hands. We have seen how folklore – our stories, customs and beliefs – can help us look at our world with fresh eyes. We see things in ways we have never seen them before, the world reframed by our myths and legends: we can see it anew as it is brought to life, watching the magic with which it has been imbued for millennia with the wonder and awe it deserves.

So, finally, after traversing the lore from across the lands of the earth, we can now ask: what is the nature of water, its inherent truth and symbolism? What do the stories we choose to tell about it teach us about ourselves?

Before we were human, our primordial ancestors came from the seas. Before we are born, we are sustained by the fluid that surrounded our developing forms in the womb. Water flows in our blood. It is part of us, one with us. Water gives us life. Water *is* life. Then – in our Underworld tales – it helps transport us to death, purifying us, and cleansing us of our human ills with our rituals. Water, for many, represents human emotion: bubbling, boiling and gushing, or flowing serenely through us, still as a calm pool.

By looking at the similarities of sea and river lore from around the world, we see an inherent truth to humanity worldwide: that many of our fears and dreams are the same, no matter who we are or where we come from. The waters of the earth course through our very veins; it is the essence of life that we cannot do without. And when we, as humans, are brave – or foolhardy – enough to gaze upon its mysteries, we see our very own image reflected right back up at us: tempestuous, changeable, dangerous, yet so beautiful, concealing mysteries, secret yearnings and a creative and turbulent force within our world – we are just like water itself. We look at our rivers and see the intrinsic, deep truth of our own humanity reflected back, as they course through the land leaving trails of stories behind them – just as our own lives do as we move from birth to our own deaths. And when our ebbing and flowing journeys are over, we will rejoin with the earth once more at our end – in the same way that rivers one day meet the sea, pouring all of their magic and mystery back into the blue beyond.

Acknowledgements

As with all books, this one would not have been possible without the help of so many special people.

We'd like to thank everyone in the #FolkloreThursday community for their continued support and enthusiasm since we started in 2015. We'd like to thank especially the hashtag hosts for running the #FolkloreThursday hashtag day on Twitter each Thursday, the editing and web team for helping to keep the website in shape, and to all of those who have contributed articles to FolkloreThursday.com over the years. We also couldn't have managed to keep things running without the support we've received from our Patreon sponsors, so a huge thanks goes out to all of you.

Thank you also to our wonderful families, our nearest and dearest who have seen us through the process from initial dream to making this book a reality.

We'd like to give a special thanks to Shanon Sinn, author of *The Haunting of Vancouver Island*, and Rosaria Tundo for their help with fact checking and proofreading. Also to staff at the Church of the Latter Day Saints Church History Library for providing access to documents that have aided in our research. Finally, a thank you to the whole Batsford team, and everyone over at Sprung Sultan for their support throughout the entire process.

Author's note

In this collection of customs and stories, we have tried to build bridges between people from all places. We wanted to show how humankind tells similar tales of the waves wherever they are from. In order to do this, we have unearthed stories from across the globe and gathered them together here. Many of the stories in this book were chosen to highlight this issue of cultural appropriation, and we have tried to explain how such stories have been appropriated, and the damage that this does.

With this in mind, we have tried to use sources from the culture each tale or tradition originates, preserving the essence of the tale in language that would be familiar to those who share its heritage. And while it is sometimes more difficult for the reader, we have used the names people call themselves. It is a mark of respect and acknowledgment that these stories belong somewhere, and belong to the people of that place. For traditions and stories from living traditions, we have made sure to use the present tense, and not erroneously mark these as a thing that is past. Folklore refers just as much to the living, breathing folk groups and customs we see all around us today. We have chosen to use the term 'sacred story', to acknowledge that many see 'myth' as something false.

We have purposefully chosen folklore that uncovers the similarities between the different cultures in humanity. Yet we have preserved the details of each tale, in hope to display the intricate details that make each folk group so mesmerisingly different to evoke the places where this lore originates, and celebrate their individuality.

We would like to thank everyone who has shared their tales and traditions with us, and we hope we have done justice to the wonderful lore that unites us all.

References

Part One – Treasures, Seduction and Death: The Lure of the Ocean Waves

The Seas and Oceans

Blennerhassett, K., *Sara la Kali: The Mysterious Saint Loved by the Gypsies*, 2014, https://www.bbc.co.uk/programmes/p0227g8h (accessed 15/3/17)

Strabo's *Geography* 7.3.6, referencing Callimachus' account in relation to Euhemerus; also, *Bradford, Ernle, Ulysses Found,* Harcourt, Brace & World, 1963

Up Helly Aa, http://www.uphellyaa.org/

Famous Floods

Flood, Josephine, *Archaeology of the Dreamtime,* Honolulu, University of Hawaii Press, 1983

Gaster, T.H., *Myth, Legend, and Custom in the Old Testament,* New York, Harper & Row, 1969

Holmberg, Uno, 'Finno-Ugric, Siberian', in MacCulloch, C.J.A. (ed.), *The Mythology of All Races,* Vol. IV, Boston, Marshall Jones Co. 1927, pp. 318–73

Kahler-Meyer, Emmi, 'Myth Motifs in Flood Stories from the Grasslands of Cameroon', in Dundes, Alan (ed.), *The Flood Myth*, Berkeley and London, University of California Press, 1988

Karahashi, F. and López-Ruiz, C., 'Love Rejected: Some Notes on the Mesopotamian "Epic of Gilgamesh" and the Greek Myth of "Hippolytus"', *Journal of Cuneiform Studies*, 2006, Vol. 58, pp. 97–107

Kolig, Erich, 'Noah's Ark Revisited: On the Myth-Land Connection in Traditional Australian Aboriginal Thought', in Dundes, Alan (ed.), *The Flood Myth*, Berkeley and London, University of California Press, 1988

Lambert, W.G., 'Berossus and Babylonian Eschatology', *Iraq,* Vol. 38 No. 2, Autumn 1976, p. 172

Miller, Hugh, *The Testimony of the Rocks, Or, Geology in Its Bearings on the Two Theologies, Natural and Revealed,* Boston, Gould and Lincoln, 1857

Sandars, N.K. (transl.), *The Epic of Gilgamesh*, Harmondsworth, Penguin Books Ltd, 1972

Sturluson, S., *The Prose Edda*, Byock, J.L. (transl.), London, Penguin, 2005

Mermaids, Selkies, and Sirens

Seductress or Saviour? The Timeless Lure of the Mermaid

Columbus, Christopher, *The journal of Christopher Columbus (during his first voyage, 1492–93) and documents relating to the voyages of John Cabot and Gaspar Corte Real,* London, 1893

Dow, James R., and Mercatante, Anthony S., *The Facts on File Encyclopedia of World Mythology and Legend,* Facts on File, 2009

Hunt, Robert, *Popular Romances of the West of England*, London, Chatto and Windus, 3rd edition, 1908

Mouritsen, Lone, *The Rough Guide to Copenhagen*, 2010, also http://www.denmark.net/denmark-guide/attractions-denmark/little-mermaid-copenhagen/

Oldfather, C.H., *The Library of History of Diodorus Siculus,* Vol. I Book 2 (Loeb Classical Library edition), 1933 (interestingly, Atargatis has been identified with the goddess Derceto, and is believed to be one and the same)

The Little Mermaid: A Tale from Denmark

Andersen, H.C., *Fairy Tales from Hans Christian Andersen*, London, 1906, pp. 1-21

The King of Humbug: P.T. Barnum and the Feejee Mermaid

Levi, S.C., 'P.T. Barnum and the Feejee Mermaid', *Western Folklore,* Vol. 36 No. 2, 1977, pp. 149–54

The Call of the Siren

Butler, S. (transl.), *The Odyssey of Homer, Book XII*, New York, Walter J. Black, 1944

Charles, R.H. (transl.), *The Book of Enoch*, London, 1917

Papoutsakis, Manolis, 'Ostriches into Sirens: Towards an Understanding of a Septuagint Crux', *Journal of Jewish Studies,* Vol. iv No. 1, Spring 2004, pp. 25–36

Vinycomb, J., *Fictitious and Symbolic Creatures in Art*, London, 1906

The Selkie-folk, the Shapeshifting Seals of the Northern Seas

Child, F.J., *The English and Scottish Popular Ballads*: 113, 1882–1898 http://www.sacred-texts.com/neu/eng/child/ch113.htm (accessed 15/02/17)

Traill Dennison, W., 'Orkney Folk-Lore', in *The Scottish Antiquary, or, Northern Notes and Queries,* Vol. 7 No. 28, Edinburgh University Press, 1893

From Mermaid to Serpent Queen: The Many Guises of Mami Wata

Drewal, H.J., 'Performing the Other: Mami Wata Worship in Africa', *TDR* (1988–), Vol. 32 No. 2, Summer 1988, pp. 160–85, The MIT Press, https://www.jstor.org/stable/pdf/1145857.pdf (accessed 12/12/19)

Drewal, H.J., 'Mami Wata: Arts for Water Spirits in Africa and Its Diasporas', *African Arts,* Summer 2008

Iroegbu, Patrick, *Healing Insanity: a Study of Igbo Medicine in Contemporary Nigeria,* Xlibris, 2010

Kameir, Rawiya, '7 Artists Explain The Significance Of The Goddess That Inspired Lemonade', *Fader,* 26 May 2016, https://www.thefader.com/2016/05/26/mami-wata-goddess-exhibition-knockdown-center (accessed: 13/12/19)

The Fabled Coast of Puglia

The Legend of Cristalda and Pizzomunno

D'Addetta, Giuseppe, 'Ogni cento anni', La Tribuna di Foggia, October 18, 1954, full text available from Ragno, Anna M., 'Da "Vieste la sperduta" alla leggenda di Cristalda e Pizzomunno cantata da Max Gazzè', *Viestane Stories,* http://storieviestane.blogspot.com/2018/02/da-vieste-la-sperduta-alla-leggenda-di.html (accessed 13/12/19)

Lattanzi, Antonella, 'Sanremo 2018, la leggenda di Cristalda e Pizzomunno: ecco l'amore eterno cantato da Max Gazzè', *La Repubblica,* 7 February 2018,

https://bari.repubblica.it/cronaca/2018/02/07/news/sanremo_2018_come_nasce_la_leggenda_di_cristalda_e_pizzomunno_max_gazze_canta_l_amore_eterno-188242301(accessed 13/12/19)

The Dolphin of Taranto

Hruby, Denise and Cristofoletti, Thomas, 'Families fight against toxic dust from Italy's Ilva steelworks', BBC, 17 September 2019, https://www.bbc.co.uk/news/world-europe-49713147 (accessed 12/12/19)

Malkin, Irad, *Myth and Territory in the Spartan Mediterranean,* New York: Cambridge University Press, 1994, p. 133

Pausanias, *Description of Greece* 10. 10. 8 https://www.theoi.com/Text/Pausanias10A.html (accessed 12/12/19)

Sneakers76 website, https://www.sneakers76.com/en/puma/900-puma-x-sneakers76-10th-anniversary-blaze-of-glory-soft-the-legend-of-dolphin-363057-001.html

The Priestess Io and the Ionian Sea

Apollodorus, *The Library,* Book 2, Translated by J.G. Frazer, 2.1.3, http://www.perseus.tufts.edu/hopper/

Monsters from the Deep

Dalley, S., *Myths from Mesopotamia,* Oxford University Press, 1987, p. 329

Enuma Elish, Tablet IV, lines 104–5, 137–8, 144, from Heidel, *Babylonian Genesis,* pp. 41–42

Job 41:14–34, *The King James Bible,* https://www.kingjamesbibleonline.org/Job-Chapter-41/ (accessed 14/2/17)

Kennedy, M., *U-boat wreck could be sea monster victim of internet folklore,* 19 October 2016, https://www.theguardian.com/world/2016/oct/19/u-boat-wreck-could-be-sea-monster-victim-of-internet-folklore (accessed 14/2/17)

National Geographic Society, *Giant Squid*, 1996–2015, http://www.nationalgeographic.com/animals/invertebrates/g/giant-squid/ (accessed 14/2/17)

Pontoppidan, E., *Natural History of Norway,* 1755, pp. 210–14, https://play.google.com/books/reader?id=3OglUqRf_soC&printsec=frontcover&output=reader&hl=en&pg=GBS.RA1-PA210 (accessed 14/2/17)

Rodkinson, M.L. (transl.), *Babylonian Talmud, Book 7: Tract Baba Bathra (Last Gate),* 1918, http://www.sacred-texts.com/jud/t07/t0709.htm (accessed 14/2/17)

Sturluson, S. (trans. Jesse L. Byock), *The Prose Edda,* London, Penguin, 2005, p. 38

Scylla and Charybdis

Bulfinch, T., 'Scylla and Charybdis', *Bulfinch's Mythology: The Age of Fable,* Chapter 28, 1855, http://www.sacred-texts.com/cla/bulf/bulf28.htm (accessed 01/02/17)

Butler, S., 'Book XII', *The Odyssey of Homer,* 1900, http://www.sacred-texts.com/cla/homer/ody/ody12.htm (accessed 01/02/17)

Ogden, Daniel, *Drakon: Dragon Myth and Serpent Cult in the Greek and Roman Worlds,* Oxford University Press, 2013

Ovid (transl. John Dryden, *et al*), 'The Voyage of Aeneas', in *Metamorphoses XIII,* 1717, http://sacred-texts.com/cla/ovid/meta/meta13.htm (accessed 30/1/17)

Ovid (transl. John Dryden, *et al*), 'The Story of Glaucus and Scylla', in *Metamorphoses XIII,* 1717, http://sacred-texts.com/cla/ovid/meta/meta13.htm (accessed 30/1/17)

Ovid (transl. John Dryden, *et al*), 'The Transformation of Scylla', in *Metamorphoses*

XIII, 1717, http://sacred-texts.com/cla/ovid/meta/meta13.htm (accessed 30/1/17)

Virgil, 'Scylla and Charybdis, the Rocks', *Æneid, Book III*, Verse 12, translated by C.P. Cranch, http://www.bartleby.com/270/5/342.html (accessed 01/02/17)

Islands of Fable and Myth

Bunin, Ivan and Bowie, Robert (transl.), *Night of Denial: Stories and Novellas*, Northwest University Press, 2006, p. 555, also *Slavic and East European Journal,* No. 3, 1989, p. 438

Pushkin, A., Zellikoff, Louis (transl.), *The Tale of Tsar Saltan,* 1905

Ralston, W.R.S., *Songs of the Russian People*, New York, 1872, p. 368, p. 376

Ralston, W R S, *Russian Fairy Tales, A Choice Collection of Muscovite Folklore*, New York, 1887, pp. 119–20

Skyes, E., Kendall, A, *Who's Who in Non-Classical Mythology*, London, Routledge, 2001

Maui, Demi-God and Creator of Islands

Dixon, Roland B., *Oceanic Mythology,* Boston, 1916, p. 44

Westervelt, W.D., *Legends of Ma-ui – A Demi God of Polynesia and of his mother Hina*, The Hawaiian Gazette Co. Ltd, 1910, p.vi

Claimed by the Waves: The Lost City of Ys

Doan, James, 'The Legend of the Sunken City in Welsh and Breton Tradition', *Folklore,* Vol. 92 No. 1, 1981, pp. 77–83

Goddio, Franck, *Topography and Excavation of Heracleion-Thonis and East Canopus (1996–2006)*, Oxford Centre for Maritime Archaeology, 2007

Guyot, Charles (transl. Deirdre Cavanagh), *The Legend of the City of Ys*, Amherst, University of Massachusetts Press, 1979

McCarthy, D.F. (ed.), *The Book of Irish Ballads*, Dublin, 1846, p. 48

Plato (transl. B. Jowett), *Timaeus,* 2008

Plato (transl. B. Jowett), *Critias,* 2008

Varin, Amy, 'Dahut and Gradlon', *Proceedings of the Harvard Celtic Colloquium,* Vol. 2, 1982, pp. 19–30

Whitfield, H.J., *Scilly and Its Legends*, 1852, pp. 16–24

The German Atlantis: The Lost City of Vineta

Brysac, Shareen Blair, 'Letters from Germany: Atlantis of the Baltic', *Archaeology*, Vol. 56 No. 4, July/August, 2003, p. 62

Hubert, Jürgen, *That Sinking Feeling – The Lost City of Vineta*, 2019 https://www.patreon.com/posts/that-sinking-of-27886163

Urashima Taro and the Palace of the Dragon King

'Legend of Urashima Taro', in *Nihon Shoki* (*The Chronicles of Japan*) Scroll 14: Emperor Yúryaku, year 22, http://archive.wul.waseda.ac.jp/kosho/ri05/ri05_01940/ri05_01940_0014/ri05_01940_0014.html (accessed 08/02/17)

Otto, A.F., 'Urashima, the Japanese Rip Van Winkle', in *Mythological Japan: the symbolisms of mythology in relation to Japanese art*, Philadelphia, Drexel Biddle, 1902, p. 28, https://archive.org/stream/mythologicaljapa00otto#page/28/mode/1up/search/taro (accessed 08/02/17)

Ozaki, Yei Theodora, 'The Story of Urashima Taro, The Fisher Lad', in Ozaki, Y.T., *Japanese Fairy Tales,* New York, A.L. Burt Company 1908, http://etc.usf.edu/lit2go/72/japanese-fairy-tales/4881/the-story-of-urashima-taro-the-fisher-lad/ (accessed 08/02/17)

Scheherazade's Tales: One Thousand and One Nights

The Fisherman and the Jinni

Burton, Richard, 'The Fisherman and the Jinni', *The Arabian Nights*, 1850, https://middleeast.library.cornell.edu/content/fisherman-and-jinni (accessed 09/11/2019)

The Tale of the Ensorcelled Prince

Burton, Richard, 'The Tale of the Ensorcelled Prince', *The Arabian Nights*, 1850, https://middleeast.library.cornell.edu/content/tale-ensorceled-prince (accessed 09/11/2019).

Reversal of Fortune: The Lady of Stavoren

Griffis, W.E. (transl.), *Dutch Fairy Tales for Young Folks: 21 Illustrated Children's Stories,* Abela Publishing, 2018

Ritchie, Leitch, *Travelling Sketches on the Rhine, and in Belgium and Holland,* Longman, 1833

Top Seven Tales from the Seven Seas

Boaz, F., 'The Central Eskimo', *Sixth Annual Report of the Bureau of Ethnology to the Secretary of the Smithsonian Institution, 1884–1885,* Washington, Government Printing Office, 1888, pp. 399-670 http://gutenberg.readingroo.ms/4/2/0/8/42084/42084-h/42084-h.htm (accessed 23/09/17)

De Shong Meador, B. (ed.), *Inanna, Lady of Largest Heart: Poems of the Sumerian High Priestess Enheduanna*, Austin, University of Texas, 2001

Eugenio, D.L. (ed.), *Philippine Folk Literature: An Anthology*, Quezon City, University of the Philippines Press, 2007

Florek, S., *Creation Story from Lake Toba, Sumatra, Indonesia,* 2012, https://australianmuseum.net.au/creation-story-from-lake-toba-sumatra-indonesia, (accessed 23/09/17)

Harris, P., Matamua, R., Smith, T., Kerr, H. & Waaka, T., 'A review of Māori astronomy in Aotearoa-New Zealand' in *Journal of Astronomical History and Heritage*, 16(3), 325–336 (2013), https://pdfs.semanticscholar.org/e875/4b1a81d4b53433b36f272a1f76709f836f5e.pdf (accessed 28/12/19)

Hutching, Gerard, 'Sharks and rays - Maori and sharks', *Te Ara – the Encyclopedia of New Zealand*, http://www.TeAra.govt.nz/en/sharks-and-rays/page-2 (accessed 28/12/19)

Knappert, J. (ed. and transl.), *Bantu Myths and Other Tales*, Leiden, E.J. Brill, 1977

Monaghan, P., *Encyclopedia of Goddesses and Heroines,* California, New World Library, 2014

Morphy, R., 'The Ningen: Myth, Monster or Make Believe?', 2011, http://mysteriousuniverse.org/2011/08/the-ningen-myth-monster-or-make-believe/ (accessed 23/09/17)

Newell Wardle, H., 'The Sedna Cycle: A Study in Myth Evolution', *American Anthropologist New Serie,s* Vol. 2 No. 3 (Jul.–Sep. 1900), p. 574, http://www.jstor.org/stable/658969 (accessed 08/02/17)

Red Sky at Night: Sailor Superstitions from Across the Globe

Bassett, Fletcher, *Legends and Superstitions of the Sea and Sailors*, Belford, Clarke and Co., Chicago, 1885, p. 442

Omisdsalar, M., 'Cat I. In Mythology and Folklore', *Encyclopedia Iranica,* 15 December 1990, http://www.iranicaonline.org/articles/cat-in-mythology-and-folklore-khot (accessed: 23/09/2017)

West, E.W. (transl.), *Pahlavi texts, part 2,* 1882, p. 419, https://www.sacred-texts.com/zor/sbe18/ sbe18125.htm (accessed 13/10/2017

Haunting the Waves: Ghostly Ships and Skeleton Crews

Birchell, C., *Sea Breezes: The Ship Lovers' Digest,* Vol. 74 2000, p.51; also Ourang – CIA Letter – https://www.cia.gov/library/readingroom/docs/CIA-RDP80R01731R000300010043-5.pdf (retrieved: 23/09/2017)

Febles, Jorge, *Into the Mainstream: Essays on Spanish American and Latino Literature and Culture,* Cambridge Scholars Publishing, 2009, pp. 202–13

Hicks, Brian, *Ghost Ship: The Mysterious True Story of the Mary Celeste and Her Missing Crew,* Random House, 2004, pp. 4–5

The Graveyard of the Atlantic: The Mystery of the Bermuda Triangle

Gaddis, Vincent H., 'The Deadly Bermuda Triangle', *Argosy* Magazine, February 1964

Jones, E.V.W., 'Sea's Puzzles Still Baffle Men in Pushbutton Age', *Miami Herald,* 17 September 1950, p. 6

Of Coffins, Rogues and Priests: Smuggling Around England's Coasts

Baring-Gould, Sabine, *The Vicar of Morwenstow, a life of Robert Stephen Hawker,* London, 1876

Baring-Gould, Sabine, *A Book of the West,* London, 1900, p. 366

Egerton, John Coker, *The Story of Sussex,* Hove, 1920, p. 274

Kingshill, Sophia and Westwood, Jennifer, *The Fabled Coast,* Random House, 2012, p. 68

Lucas, E.V., *Highways and Byways in Sussex*, London, 1904, p. 274

Waugh, Mary, *Smuggling in Devon and Cornwall, 1700–1850*, Countryside Books, 1991, p. 41

Part Two – What Lurks Beneath: Sacred Rivers and Mysterious Lakes

Rivers and Lakes

Äikäs, Tiina, 'From Boulders to Fells Sacred Places in the Sámi Ritual Landscape', *Monographs of the Archaeological Society of Finland, 2015,* http://www.academia.edu/17988252/From_Boulders_to_Fells_Sacred_Places_in_the_Sámi_Ritual_Landscape (accessed 10/12/18)

Grimm, Jacob, *Teutonic Mythology*, Vol. 2 (transl. Stallybrass, James Steven), London: George Bell & Sons, 1883, p. 496, https://archive.org/details/teutonicmytholo02grim/page/494 (accessed 13/11/18)

Larrington, Carolyne (transl.), *The Poetic Edda*, 2nd ed., Oxford University Press, 2014, p. 284

Sacred Rivers

Alter, Stephen, *Sacred Waters: A Pilgrimage Up the Ganga River to the Source of Hindu Culture*, Houghton Mifflin Harcourt, Trade & Reference Publishers, 2001

Baynes, C., 'Gangasagar Ritual: When is the Hindu ritual, and what happens during it?', in *The Independent*, 18 January 2018, https://www.independent.co.uk/news/world/asia/gangasagar-pilgrimage-what-happens-when-meaning-hindu-ritual-india-ganges-a8152411.html (accessed 15/06/18)

Bhattacharji, Sukumari and Bandyopadhyay, Ramananda, *Legends of Devi*, Orient Blackswan, 1995

Davison, I., 'Whanganui River given legal status of a person under unique Treaty of Waitangi settlement', *The New Zealand Herald,* 15 March 2017, https://www.nzherald.co.nz/nz/news/article.cfm?c_id=1&objectid=11818858 (accessed 11/06/18)

Rice, Earle, *The Ganges River,* Mitchell Lane Publishers Inc., 2012, p. 25

Upadhyay, V., 'Ganga, Yamuna are "living persons with legal rights": High court', *Times of India*, 20 March 2017, https://timesofindia.indiatimes.com/city/dehradun/ganga-yamuna-are-living-persons-with-legal-rights-hc/articleshow/57739429.cms (accessed 11/06/18)

Urton, Gary, *At the Crossroads of the Earth and the Sky – An Andean Cosmology,* University of Texas Press, Austin, 1981

Rivers of the Underworld

Aristophanes, *Frogs* (Matthew Dillon, ed.) pp.185–6, http://www.perseus.tufts.edu/hopper/text?doc=Perseus%3Atext%3A1999.01.0032%3Acard%3D185

Christenson, Allen J., *Popol Vuh: The Sacred Book of the Maya*, Vol. 1, University of Oklahoma Press, 2003, p. 95

'Grímnismál' 28, *Poetic Edda,* http://www.sacred-texts.com/neu/poe/poe06.htm (accessed 16/04/18)

Jones, W.H.S (transl.), 'Description Of Greece: Nonacris & River Styx', *Pausanias* 8.18, http://www.theoi.com/Text/Pausanias8B.html (accessed 16/04/18)

Leeming, David, 'Styx', The Oxford Companion to World Mythology, Oxford University Press, http://www.oxfordreference.com/view/10.1093/acref/9780195156690.001.0001/acref-9780195156690-e-1497?rskey=rTReql&result=1320&q (accessed 17/04/18)

Lindow, John, *Norse Mythology: A Guide to Gods, Heroes, Rituals, and Beliefs*, Oxford University Press, 2002, p. 142

Mirto, Maria Serena and Osborne, A.M., *Death in the Greek World: From Homer to the Classical Age*, Normal: University of Oklahoma Press, 2012, p. 16

Ovid, *Metamorphoses,* vii.4

Ruud, Martin B., 'The Draumkvæde: A Norwegian Vision Poem of the Thirteenth Century', *Scandinavian Studies and Notes*, Vol. 7, pp. 53–4, https://archive.org/stream/jstor-40915098/40915098_djvu.txt (accessed: 16/04/18)

Scharfe, Hartmut, 'The sacred water of the Ganges and the Styx-water', in *Zeitschrift für vergleichende Sprachforschung* 86. Bd.1. H. (1972), pp. 116–20, http://www.jstor.org/stable/40849437 (accessed 16/04/2018)

Sturluson, Snorri, 13th century, 'Gylfaginning', in the *Prose Edda*, http://www.sacred-texts.com/neu/pre/pre04.htm (accessed 16/04/18)

Tregear, Edward, 1891, *Maori-Polynesian Comparative Dictionary*, Wellington: Government Printer, p. 322, https://archive.org/details/maoripolynesian01treggoog (accessed 17/05/18)

Various translators, *The Suda Online: Byzantine Lexicography,* 2000, https://www.cs.uky.edu/~raphael/sol/sol-html/ (accessed 06/04/18)

Virgil, *Aeneid Book VI,* translated by William Hutton, 2000, http://www.theoi.com/Text/VirgilAeneid6.html (accessed 09/05/2017)

'Völuspá', stanzas 59–66, from *The Poetic Edda*, by Henry Adams Bellows, 1936, p. 2, http://www.sacred-texts.com/neu/poe/poe03.htm (accessed 17/05/18)

Forgotten Waters: The Hidden Rivers of London

Barton, Nicholas, *The Lost Rivers of London,* Historical Publications, 2016, p. 80

Bolton, Tom, *London's Lost Rivers: A Walker's Guide,* Strange Attractor Press, London, 2011, p. 34

Foord, Alfred Stanley, *Springs, Streams and Spas of London; history and associations*, New York, 1910, p. 49

Newman, Jon, *River Effra: South London's Secret Spine,* Signal Books, 2016

O'Donnell, Elliott, *Haunted Waters*, Rider and Company, London, 1957, p. 140

Roud, Steve, *London Lore,* Arrow Books, 2010, p. 19

Talling, Paul, *London's Lost Rivers*, https://www.londonslostrivers.com (accessed 25/11/18)

Waterfall Folklore

The Maid of the Mist

Aichele, K. Porter, 1984, 'The "Spirit of Niagara": Success or Failure?', in *Art Journal*, 44(1), 46–49, JSTOR, www.jstor.org/stable/776673. (accessed 24/10/18)

Carmer, Carl, *Three Centuries of Niagara Falls*, Buffalo, NY: Albright-Knox Art Gallery, 1964, p. 56

Kirkey, Sharon, '"I feel like it's pulling me": The suicidal trance of Niagara Falls', *OttowaCitizen.com*, 20 February 2018 https://ottawacitizen.com/news/the-dangerous-trance-of-niagara-falls/wcm/f8027fd7-3b7e-4601-82c9-0e4e836ad34d (accessed 24/10/18)

Morgan, Lewis Henry, *League of the Ho-dé-no-sau-nee, or Iroquois*, Rochester: Sage & Brother, New York: M.H. Newman & Co., 1851, pp. 158–60, https://archive.org/details/leagueofhodnos00inmorg/page/158 (accessed 30/10/18)

The Dragon's Gate

De Visser, M.W., 2008, *The Dragon in China and Japan*, p. 86

Oba's Ear: A Tale of the Yoruba River Spirit

Bascom, William, 'Oba's Ear: A Yoruba Myth in Cuba and Brazil' in *Research in African Literatures*, Vol. 7, No. 2 (Autumn 1976), pp. 149–65

González-Wippler and Migene, *Santeria: The Religion*, Llewellyn, 1994

Irele, Abiola,Jeyifo, Biodun, eds., *The Oxford Encyclopedia of African Thought*, Vol. 1, Oxford University Press, 2010, p. 305

The Top Five River Spirits from Around the World

Apollodorus, *The Library of Apollodorus* 3.12.3, Sir James George Frazer (ed.), Delphi Classics, 2016, https://books.google.it/books?id=eFm-QCwAAQBAJ&pg=PT235&lpg=PT235&dq=Scholiast+on+Lyco-phron+355&source=bl&ots=c-x8OspOKB&sig=uuh5DuOPURX-O5maqZRKzhA07blQ&hl=en&sa=X&ved=2ahUKEwjksNuAj8LeAhUP-2BoKHVcPBMEQ6AEwAHoECAkQAQ#v=onepage&q=pallas&f=false (accessed 07/11/18)

Baring-Gould, S. (Sabine), *Curious myths of the Middle Ages*, London, Rivingtons

Couldrette, 14th/15th century, Skeat, Walter W. (Walter William), *The Romans of Partenay, or of Lusignen: otherwise known as the Tale of Melusine*, London, N. Trübner & Co., 1866, https://archive.org/details/romanspartenayo00coulgoog (accessed 06/11/18)

Grimm, Jacob, *Teutonic Mythology,* 4th edition (transl. James Stallybrass), Vol. 2, London, Bell, 1883, pp. 492–3

Herodotus, *The Histories, 4. 180, 1–4*, Vol. 2, translated by A.D. Godley, Cambridge, Harvard University Press, 1920, https://archive.org/details/herodotuswitheng02herouoft/page/380 (accessed 07/11/19)

Thorpe, Benjamin, *Northern Mythology: comprising the principal popular traditions and superstitions of Scandinavia, north Germany, and the Netherlands*, 3 vols, London, Lumley, 1851–52, Vol. 2, Scandinavian Popular Traditions and

Superstitions, p. 23, https://archive.org/details/northernmytholog02thor (accessed 02/11/18)

Sébillot, Paul, *Le Folk-Lore de la France: La Mer et les Eaux Douces – Tome deuxième*, Ligaran, 1905, pp. 345–6, https://archive.org/stream/lefolkloredefran02sbuoft/lefolkloredefran02sbuoft_djvu.txt (accessed 02/11/18)

Vanin, Adriano, *Il regno dei Fanes. Analisi di una leggenda delle Dolomiti*, Il Cerchio, 2013; 'The "anguine"', *The Fanes' saga – Short essays,* http://www.ilregnodeifanes.it/inglese/essay1.htm (accessed: 02/11/18)

Wolff, Karl Felix, *Il regno dei Fanes*, Cappelli, 1951, Bologna

The Mysterious Waters of Scotland

Briggs, Katharine, *An Encyclopedia of Fairies*, Pantheon, 1976, pp. 19–20

Campbell, John Gregorson, *Superstitions of the Highlands and Islands of Scotland*, Glasgow, 1900, p. 44

Douglas, George, *Scottish Fairy and Folk Tales*, Dover Publications, 2003

Henderson, George, *Survivals in Belief Among the Celts*, Glasgow, 1911

Water Horses: Majestic and Malevolent Creatures from the Depths

Gregor, Revd Walter, *Notes on the Folk-Lore of the North-East of Scotland*, London, 1881, p. 66

London, John, *Swedish Legends and Folktales*, Berkeley, University of California Press, p. 121

Trevelyan, Marie, *Folklore and Folk-Stories of Wales*, London, 1909, p. 61

Humped Serpents and Vicious Eels: Loch Ness and the World's Most Fearsome Lake Monsters

Abraham Ortelius's map of Iceland, detail around Lagarfljót showing the inscription, https://en.wikipedia.org/wiki/Lagarflj%C3%B3t_Worm#/media/File:Lagarfljot-ortelius_(1585)_-with-position.jpg (accessed 12/1/2020)

Arnanson, J. and Simpson, J., transl., *Icelandic Folktales and Legends*, University of California Press, 1972, p. 103

Beaver, Trish, *What is the Howick Falls Monster – a myth or popular folklore*, 15 July 2013, https://howickvillage.co.za/news/1197-what-is-the-howick-falls-monster-a-myth-or-popular-folklore (accessed: 19/10/2018)

Fordred-Green, Lesley, 'Tokoloshe Tales: Reflections on the Cultural Politics of Journalism in South Africa', *Current Anthropology*, Vol. 41, No. 5, December 2000, p. 702, https://web.archive.org/web/20060113075226/http://www.

getawaytoafrica.com/content/magazine/features/feature.asp?id=909

Huyshe, Wentworth (transl.), *The Life of St Columba by St Adamnan*, London, 1905

legendenglishupf, *The legend of the monster of the Lake in Banyoles*, 13 Februry 2013, https://legendenglishupf.wordpress.com/2013/02/13/the-legend-of-the-monster-of-the-lake-in-banyoles-why-people-in-banyoles-can-swim-in-the-lake/ (accessed: 8/5/2018)

Ogopogo

Gaal, Arlene, *In Search of Ogopogo: Sacred Creature of the Okanagan Waters*, Hancock House Publishers, 2019, p. 88

Radford, Benjamin, *Ogopogo: Canada's Loch Ness Monster*, 8 January 2014, https://www.livescience.com/42399-ogopogo.html (accessed. 12/7/2018)

Van Eijk, Jan P., 'Who Is Súnułqaz'?: A Salish Quest', *Anthropological Linguistics*, Vol. 43, No. 2 (Summer 2001), p. 193

Folklore or Fakelore? The Monster of Bear Lake

Rich, Joseph C., 'Bear Lake Monster', *Deseret News*, 27 July 1868, reprinted 6 May 1940, Utah State University, Digital History Collections, https://digital.lib.usu.edu/digital/collection/bearlakemon/id/433/ (accessed: 3/5/2018)

Rich, Joseph C., *Joseph C. Rich Addresses the People of Bear Lake Valley*, Joseph Coulson Rich Collection, Church History Library, The Church of Jesus Christ of Latter Day Saints, Salt Lake City, Utah

The Folklore of Swamps and Marshes

Cryptocrew.com, *Honey Island Swamp Monster 1963,* https://www.youtube.com/watch?v=dtXzA3oeypo (accessed 19/1018)

Geelong Advertiser, 2 July 1845, in Ravenscroft, Peter, *Bunyip and Inland Seal Archive*, https://trove.nla.gov.au/newspaper/article/94443733 (accessed: 27/09/18)

Holyfield, Dana, *Honey Island Swamp Monster Official Website*, http://www.angelfire.com/la2/SwampMonster/ (accessed 19/10/18)

'Honey Island Swamp Monster', original clip from *Hannity's America,* aired on Fox News Channel between 2007 and 2009, https://www.youtube.com/watch?v=4w-GOleG1es (accessed 19/10/18)

Morgan, John, *The Life and Adventures of William Buckley: Thirty-two Years a Wanderer,* A Macdougall, 1852, pp. 48, 108–9, https://archive.org/details/lifeandadventur00morggoog/page/n6 (accessed 07/11/18)

Thompson, Dave, *Bayou Underground: Tracing the Mythical Roots of American Popular Music*, E.C.W. Press, 2010, https://books.

google.it/books?id=4HFYKKVMvxcC&pg=PT292&redir_esc=y#v=onepage&q=letiche&f=false (accessed 19/10/18)

Workers of the Writers' Program of the Work Projects Administration in the State of Louisiana, *Louisiana: A Guide to the State*, New York: US History Publishers, 1941, https://books.google.it/books?id=lOSvzYLs3tMC&pg=PA94&redir_esc=y#v=onepage&q&f=false (accessed 19/10/18)

Sinister Bog Lights: Will-O'-the-Wisp

Ashliman, D.L. (ed.), *Will o'-the-Wisp* (2009–2019), https://www.pitt.edu/~dash/willowisp.html (accessed: 27/3/18)

Stewart, William Grant, *The Popular Superstitions and Festive Amusements of the Highlanders of Scotland*, 1823, pp. 161–2

Telangana Today, *Ghost Lights of Aleya,* 28 April 2017, https://telanganatoday.com/ghost-lights-aleya (accessed: 14/2/2018)

Be Careful Where You Rest: The Insatiable Appetite of the Irish Joint Eater

Briggs, Katharine, *An Encyclopedia of Fairies*, Pantheon Books, 1976, p. 243

Hyde, Douglas, *Beside the Fire: A Collection of Irish Gaelic Folk Stories,* London, 1890, pp. 47–73

The Shapeshifting Pink Dolphin of the Amazon River

Bates, H.W., *The Naturalist on the River Amazons: A Record of Adventures, Habits of Animals, and Aspects of Nature under the Equator, during Eleven Years of Travel,* New York, 1988, p. 291

Cravalho, M.A., 'Shameless Creatures: An Ethnozoology of the Amazon River Dolphin', in *Ethnology,* Vol. 38, No. 1, 1999, pp. 47–58, http://www.jstor.org/stable/3774086

Slater, C., *Dance of the Dolphin, Transformation and Disenchantment in the Amazonian Imagination,* Chicago, 1994, pp. 60, 66

World Wildlife Fund, 2018, 'Amazon River Dolphin', on www.worldwildlife.org, https://www.worldwildlife.org/species/amazon-river-dolphin (accessed 13/03/18)

Well Folklore

Ashliman, D.L. (transl.), 'Restoring the Moon', in *Nasreddin Hodja: Tales of the Turkish Trickster,* 2001–09, https://www.pitt.edu/~dash/hodja.html#moon

Borrow, George (transl.), *The Turkish Jester; or, The Pleasantries of Cogia Nasr Eddin Effendi*, Ipswich, W. Webber, 1884

Chainey, Dee Dee, *A Treasury of British Folklore: Maypoles, Mandrakes and Mistletoe,* London, National Trust Books, 2018, p. 35

Davidson, Linda Kay and Gitlitz, David Martin, *Pilgrimage: From the Ganges to Graceland: an Encyclopedia*, Vol. 1, ABC-CLIO, 2002, p. 358, https://books.google.it/books/about/Pilgrimage.html?id=YVYkrNhPMQkC&redir_esc=y (accessed 20/6/18)

Davis, Hazel, 'The village that lights up for the Moonraking Festival', *The Telegraph*, 17 June 2016, https://www.telegraph.co.uk/only-in-britain/village-lights-up-for-moonraking-festival/ (accessed 14/03/2018)

Depares, R, 2015, 'Of Maltese Myths and Creatures', in *The Times of Malta,* February 2015, https://www.timesofmalta.com/articles/view/20150215/books/Of-Maltese-myths-and-creatures.556386 (accessed 19/06/18)

Harris, Joel Chandler, *Nights with Uncle Remus: Myths and Legends of the Old Plantation,* Boston, Houghton Mifflin, 1911, pp. 100–7, https://archive.org/details/nightswithuncler00harr (accessed 19/06/18)

Hole, C., *English Folklore*, London, B.T. Batsford, 1940, pp. 101–2

MacCulloch, J.A., *The Mythology of All Races*, Vol. III, Part I: The Genii, Chapter IV: Genii of Fate, 1918, p. 250, https://archive.org/stream/mythologyofall03gray#page/248/mode/2up/search/fate (accessed 15/06/18)

Mifsud, Stephan D., *The Maltese Bestiary: An Illustrated Guide to the Mythical Flora and Fauna of the Maltese Islands*, Merlin Publishers, 2014

'Naga: Hindu mythology', in *Encyclopaedia Britannica*, https://www.britannica.com/topic/naga-Hindu-mythology (accessed 20/6/18)

Reljic, Teodor, 'Better the Beasts you Know', *MaltaToday.com*, 10 November 2014, https://www.maltatoday.com.mt/arts/books/45964/better_the_beasts_you_know__stephan_d_mifsud#.WykdAiAo_IU (accessed 19/06/18)

Völuspá, http://www.sacred-texts.com/neu/poe/poe03.htm (accessed 15/06/18)

Von Schiefner, F. Anton, *Tibetan Tales Derived from Indian Sources*, W.R.S Ralston (transl.), London, Kegan Paul, Trench, Trübner and Co., 1906, No. 45, p. 353, https://archive.org/stream/tibetantalesderi00schirich#page/n7/mode/2up (accessed 19/06/18)

Zatat, Narjas, 'People are debating the casting of an Asian actor as Nagini in Fantastic Beasts', *Indy 100*, 2018, https://www.indy100.com/article/debate-casting-nagini-actress-south-korean-diversity-j-k-rowling-fantastic-beasts-8557931 (accessed 10/12/18); also Tripathi, Amish, *Twitter.com,* https://twitter.com/authoramish/status/1044947100830773249 (accessed 10/12/18)

The Fountain of Youth

Peck, Douglas T., *Misconceptions and Myths Related to the Fountain of Youth and Juan Ponce de Leon's 1513 Exploration Voyage,* http://citeseerx.ist.psu.edu/viewdoc/download?doi=10.1.1.403.8989&rep=rep1&type=pdf (accessed: 14/7/2018)

Rawlinson, George (transl.), *The History of Herodotus, The Third Book, Entitled Thalia*, 1910, p. 23

Myth and Mystery: The Lady of the Lake

De Troye, Chretien (transl. W.W. Comfort), *Lancelot, The Knight of the Cart*, p. 31, http://www.heroofcamelot.com/docs/Lancelot-Knight-of-the-Cart.pdf (accessed: 16/6/2018)

Jarman, A.O.H., 'A Note on the Possible Welsh Derivation of Viviane', *Gallica: Essays Presented to J. Heywood Thomas*, Cardiff, 1969, pp. 1–12

Lang, Andrew (ed.), *King Arthur, Tales of the Round Table*, 1902, pp. 14–15

Strachey, Sir Edward (ed.), *Le Morte D'Arthur, Sir Thomas Malory's book of King Arthur and of his noble Knights of the Round Table*, London, 1919, p. 78

Index

Acheron 111–12
Africa 35–8, 126–7, 143
Aix-en-Provence 11
alatuir 55
Alexander the Great 162
Aleya 152
alp-luachra 156
Amazon River 154
Andersen, Hans Christian 20–6
anguane 130
Antarctica 87
Arabian Nights 68–76
Arctic Ocean 80
Argus 46
Arnaquagsaq 81
Arthur 62, 105, 164–6
Assal, Lake 162
Åsteson, Olav 117
Atargatis 19–20
Athena 129–30
Atlantic Ocean 81–2
Atlantis 11, 12, 59, 95
Australia 15, 149

bäckahäst 138–40
Baldr 113
Bali 10
Bangladesh 152
Banyoles Lake 143–4
baptism 104
Barnum, P.T. 27
bathing 104, 109, 162
bean-nighe 135–6
Bear Lake, USA 145–6
Bengal 152
Bergelmir 17
Bermuda Triangle 12, 94–6
Beyoncé 38
blessings 168
Blue Men of Minch 10
boobrie 133–5
Boto Encantado 154
boundaries 104
Brazil 20, 82–3, 154
Br'er Rabbit 161
bridges 115
Bridgewater Triangle 152
Brittany 59–62
Bua Ban 125
Budapest 162
Bulgaria 160
bunyip 149
Burwash, Sussex 100
Buyan 54–5

'calenture' 12
Caleuche 92–3
Calypso 11
Cameroon 16
Canada 144–5
Canute 118
Catchpole, Bessie 98–100
cats 89–90
caul births 88
Ceffyl Dŵr 138
Charlemagne 63, 143
Charon 111–12
Charybdis 51–2
Chasa Bonpuli 112
Chiloé 92–3
China 109, 123
Christianity 104, 105
Cill Stuifin 59
Circe 51–2
cities, underwater 59–66
clergymen 100, 138
clootie wells 158
Cocytus 112
coffins 98, 118
Columbus, Christopher 20
Cornwall 20, 62, 97, 152, 158
Courbefy, France 158

Cristalda 39–42
Croatia 160
Cruel Coppinger 100–1

Dahut 60
dancing 43
Dargle Lovers 125
days of the week and luck 89
Derbyshire 157–8
Devon 97, 100–1, 152
Dickens, Charles 116, 119
dolphins 43, 106, 109, 154, 168
Dragon Gate 123
dragons 47, 65–6, 84, 123, 143
drowning, protection from 88
Durham 106

Effra River 118–19
eggs 54–5
Egypt 109
Elizabeth I 119
elves 17–18
Epic of Gilgamesh 15
Ereshkigal 110
Essex 98
evolution 168–9
Excalibur 166

fairies 130–2, 152, 156, 166
Feejee Mermaid 27
Finfolkaheem 9
Finland 153
fish 123
The Fisherman and the Jinni 68–76
Fleet River 116
floods 14–18, 78
Florida 163
The Flying Dutchman 90
fossegrim 105, 132
fountains 162–3
France 11, 59–62, 128–9, 130–2, 158
Freya 89
Friesland, Netherlands 77–8
frogs 17
Funayūre i 9

Gagana 55
Ganges 104, 109
Gangnim Doryeong 112
Garafena 55
Germany 63–4, 106
ghosts 90–3, 105, 114, 115, 116
giants 17
Gjöll 113
Glaucus 51–2
goats 16, 132
Goldmann, Klaus 64
Gozo 11
Gradlon 60–2
Granny Grylls 98
Greek myth 29–30, 43–6, 51–2, 104, 111–12, 129–30, 162
Greenland 81
Grumuduk 15
Guatemala 110
Gulliver, Isaac 97–8

Hades 104, 110, 112
harpies 110
Hawaii 56
Hé-no 120–2
Hebrides 10
Heimdall 105
Hel 117
Henggimot Lake 112
Hera 46
Hermódr 113
Herodotus 129–30, 162
Hessdalen 152
Hesse, Hermann 104
Hinduism 10, 16, 109
Hit 85
Hobby Lantern 152
Homer 29, 112
Honey Island Swamp Monster 148
Howick Falls 143
Huang He 109, 123
Huay Kaew Waterfall 125
Hunahpu 110
Hutu 110
Hvergelmir 160

Iceland 142–3
Iemanjá 11, 82–3

Ignis fatuus 150
Inanna 80
Incas 108
India 109, 157
Indian Ocean 84
Indonesia 84
inkanyamba 143
Inuit people 80–1
Io 46
Ireland 59, 104–5, 125, 156, 158
islands 54–8
Italy 39–46, 130

Jack-o'-lantern 150
Japan 9, 65–6, 106
Jean d'Arras 128
Jeju Island 112
Jenny Greenteeth 106
jinni 68–74
joint-eater 156
Jomsborg 64
Jörmungandr 48
Judaism 10–11, 47

kappa 106
kelpies 10, 137–8
koi fish 123
Korea 112, 157
Koschei 54–5
Kraken 48, 50
Krech, Günther 48–50
Kumbh Mela 109
KwaNogqaza 143

The Lady of Stavoren 77–8
Lady of the Lake 105, 164–6
Lagarfljót Worm 142–3
Lancashire 106
Lancelot 166
Leiptr 117
Lethe 112
Létiche 148
Leviathan 47
Lewis, C.S. 104
Libya 129–30
The Little Mermaid (Andersen) 20–6
Liverpool 106
Loch Ness 141–2, 146
Loki 48
London 114–19
loup-garou 148–9
Lourdes 158

The Magician's Nephew (Lewis) 104
Magindang 85
The Maid of the Mist 120–2
Majorca 106
Makar Sankranti festival 109
Malta 11, 157
Mami Wata 35–8
Marduk 47
Marfa Lights 152
Maria Enganxa 106
marshes 150–3
Mary Celeste 90
Maui 56–8, 86
Mayans 110
Melasti 10
Melusine 106, 128–9
Merlin 164–6
mermaids 9, 19–27, 35–8
Mesopotamia 15, 47, 110
mice 15–16
Micronesia 85
Midgard 48
Mímir 105, 160
mirrors 35–6, 82
Mkomazi River 143
Módgudr 113
monkeys 161
monsters 47–52, 141–6, 148–9, 157, 168
moon 160–1
Morwenstowe 100
Mula Jadi 84
Munlochy, Black Isle 158
murder 116
music 8, 105, 106, 130–2
Myanmar 17–18

Naga Padoha 84
nāgas 157
naiades 129–30
Narcissus 105

Narucnici 160
Nasreddin Hodja 160
neck 106
Neckinger River 119
New Year 11
New Zealand 56, 58, 86, 108–9
N'ha-a-itk 144–5
Niagara Falls 120–2
Nile 109
Ningen 87
nixie 106–7
Noah 14, 15–16, 17
nokken 106
Norse myth 48, 89, 105, 110, 113, 158–60
nymphs 128–30

Oba 126–7
octopus 85
Odin 17, 89, 105, 160
Odysseus 29, 52
Okanagan Lake 144–5
Oliver Twist (Dickens) 116, 119
One Thousand and One Nights 68–76
Opopogo 144–5
orishas 126–7
orixá 82–3
Orkney 9, 31, 32
Otohime Sama 65
Ourang Medan, SS 92

Pacific 85–6
Pallas 129–30
Pare 110
Pecos Bill 146
Peg Powler 106
Persephone 30, 110
Philippines 85
Phlegethon 112
pixy-lights 152
Pizzomunno 39–42
Ponce de León 162–3
Poseidon 43, 129
Puerto Rico 162–3
purification 104, 109, 111

The Rëgn de Fanes 130
The Rime of the Ancient Mariner (Coleridge) 8
Rio de Janeiro 11
rituals 167
Romani communities 11
Rosh Hashanah 10–11
Ruamano 86
Ruden, Germany 64
Russia 15, 16–17, 56
Ryújin 65

sacredness 108–9, 157, 168
Sagar Island 109
sailing, lucky days 88–9
St Catherine of Siena 126
St Christopher 105
St Columba 141
St Curidan 158
St Emeterio 144
St Eutrope 158
St Paul 11, 43
St Winwaloe 60
Sámi people 104
Santería 126–7
Sara-la-Kali 11
Satyavrata 16
Scandinavia 9, 17, 48, 104, 106, 138–40
Scheherazade 68
Scotland 133–6, 137–8, 152, 158
Scylla 51–2
Sedna 80
selikes 19
selkies 9, 31–4
Serpentine Lake, London 115
serpents 47–8
Seven Seas 80–7
Shango 126–7
shapeshifters 12, 31–2, 92, 106–7, 157
sharks 86
shellycoat 133
Shetland 11, 31
ship naming 89
Siddhartha (Hesse) 104
sirens 9, 19, 29–30, 40
Slaithwaite, Yorkshire 161

Slavic folklore 55–6
Slidell, Louisiana 148
smugglers 97–101, 161
snakes 48, 55, 122, 157
Solomon 69–70
Southern Ocean 87
Spain 143–4
spiders 43
Spunkie 152
squid 48
Staffordshire 157
Stavoren 77–8
Styx 112
submarines 48–50
Sudjenice 160
superstitions 88–93
Sussex 100
swamps 148–9
Sweden 152
symbolism 168–9

Tahitian Islands 56
The Tale of the Ensorcelled Prince 75–6
Tangaroa 86
Taranto, Italy 43–6
tattoos 123
Te Māngōroa 86
temples 11
Terrebonne Parish 148
Thailand 125
Thonis-Heracleion 62
Tiamat 47
Tibet (China) 161
Tingoi 35
Tissington, Derbyshire 157–8
treasure 153
Tristan 62
Triton 129
turtles 17, 65–6
Tyburn River 115–16

U-boats 48–50
UFOs 93, 95
Underworld 30, 80, 84, 104, 110–13, 169
Up Helly Aa 11
Urashima Tarō 65–6
Urðr, Well of 158–60
Urubamba River 108
USA 145–6, 148–9, 150, 152, 163
Utnapishtim 15

Vieste, Italy 39–42
Vikings 11, 48, 64
Vineta 63–4
Virgil 111
Vishnu 16

Walbrook River 118
Wales 138, 158
washerwomen 135
water horses 135, 137–40
water, symbolism 168–9
waterfalls 120–5
wells 116, 157–61
werewolves 148–9
Westbourne River 115
Whanganui River 108–9
whistling 89
will-o'-the-wisp 150
Wiltshire 161
wine-glasses 89
witches 18, 89–90, 92
Wolin, Poland 64
women on ships 89
World Tree 158–60

Xbalanque 110
Xibalba 110

Yamuna River 109
Yangtze 109
Yemoja 82
Yeomra 112
Ymir 17
Yorkshire 106, 161
Yoruba people 126–7
Ys 59–62

Zeus 46, 129